Church Folks

Adria Cabey

Church Folks

Copyright © 2010-2011 by Alexdrian Publishing

Dedication

This book is dedicated to Alex Cabey because God always has a plan. The biggest blessings come in small packages, and I thank God for you. You are loved beyond measure!

Table of Contents

Prologue 5

Chapter One 14

Chapter Two...19

Chapter Three...25

Chapter Four 37

Chapter Five...45

Chapter Six...56

Chapter Seven 69

Chapter Eight 76

Chapter Nine 83

Chapter Ten...92

Chapter Eleven..100

Chapter Twelve 107

Chapter Thirteen 111

Prologue

"I'll be right back," Lillian Carter told her sister Jillian as she exited the car and headed towards the store.

Jillian was too nervous to sit, so she got out of her sister's car and began to pace aimlessly around the parking lot. She was so caught up in her jumbled thoughts that she bumped into a man who was getting out of his car.

"Excuse me," Jillian mumbled without bothering to look up.

"Are you alright?" The man placed his hands on her shoulders and she got instant chills.

"Fine, I'm sorry," she finally looked up at him. Something about the way he was looking at her made her feel very uncomfortable.

"I'm Sheldon Holmes," he released her and extended his hand to shake hers.

"I'm—"

"Jillian Carter, I know," he shook her hand, never allowing their eye contact to break.

"Nice to meet you Sheldon," she removed her hand from his firm hold and took a step back.

Sheldon smiled, "you look nice today."

Jillian looked down at the periwinkle flowered sundress she was wearing, "it's my sister's."

"I was talking about more than just the dress," he cleared his throat.

"Oh," she sighed as she sized him up. He was six feet tall with dark chocolate skin and almond shaped eyes. He had thick full lips and a muscular physique.

"It's hard to believe Lillian Carter is your sister, the two of you are as different as day and night," he licked his big lips and Jillian looked down.

"So I've been told," Jillian mumbled as she looked back towards the car.

"I don't mean to be forward, but would you mind if—"

"What the hell do you think you're doing?" Lillian approached Sheldon with a hostile tone, which told Jillian it wasn't their first run-in.

"Just having a little friendly conversation that's all. That's my word," Sheldon shrugged innocently.

"Not with my baby sister you aren't," Lillian put her hands on her hips. "Sheldon I told you to stay away from my sister. She does not want you."

Sheldon looked at Jillian and she refused to look his way, "I was just saying hello to her."

"Well now you can say goodbye to her. Jillian go get in the car," Lillian pointed to the car authoritatively.

Jillian started to walk away and Sheldon grabbed her arm, "it was really nice to finally meet you. I hope we'll have a chance to talk again sometime."

Lillian watched as her sister headed to the car, and then turned back to Sheldon, "I already told you to stay away from my sister. She doesn't want you."

"Why are you so rude? You don't even know me."

"I know that you're too old to be talking to my sister and you better stay away from her."

"What if I don't?" Sheldon challenged.

"Try me and you'll see," she stood her five foot five, one-hundred and fifty pound ground and glared up at Sheldon.

"Excuse me for not trembling with fear," he huffed.

"Just leave her alone, she has enough going on in her life right now. Besides I know your type."

"And I know your type, a big mouth you can't back up."

"Listen Sheldon, my sister is only seventeen years old. There are plenty of women out here that you can mess around with just leave her alone okay?"

"You're wrong," Sheldon shook his head in stern disagreement. "There are none out there quite like Jillian."

"You sick bastard," Lillian spat. "You're probably old enough to be her daddy. You mess with my sister and there will be hell to pay!" She was losing her cool, and would not hesitate to go to blows with the six foot muscular man who stood before her when it came to her baby sister.

"Your sister can make her own decisions. Besides, I'm not out to sleep with your sister and break her heart. That's my word," there was an arrogance about Sheldon that told Lillian that no matter what she said he was not going to give up easily.

"Then what are you trying to do?" She demanded to know.

"That's for me to know and you to find out," Sheldon gave her a sly smile before he turned and walked away. "Later Lillian."

"I'll be watching you," Lillian called before storming to the car.

"What was that all about?" Jillian turned to her sister as she got in the car.

"Stay away from him," Lillian stated with finality slamming her door shut for emphasis.

"Why?"

"He's too old for you that's why."

"How old is he?"

"Thirty something, and I heard he's been asking people about you. Trust me older men have been around and they know the game and how to use it to their advantage."

"Why?" She asked with the innocence of a three year old.

Suddenly Lillian regretted her decision to be so overprotective of her little sister, "why do you think Jillian?" She gave her an icy glare.

"I don't know," Jillian shrugged innocently with a smile. "Maybe he's nice. He seemed pretty interested in me."

"The only thing that man is interested in is what's in between your legs. Keep them closed or you'll have to deal with the crap I'm dealing with," she tossed the bag with the pregnancy test she'd just purchased to her sister and cranked up the ignition.

"Man these are the longest minutes of my life," Lillian sighed as she and her sister sat in their bedroom awaiting the test results. "That's what I get for being cheap. I should have bought the more expensive one and been done with this."

"I think I need to throw up," Jillian tried to stand and Lillian pulled her back down.

"What are you having sympathy symptoms?" Lillian laughed.

"This is not funny," Jillian huffed.

"You're right…look," Lillian turned the applicator with the result in her sister's direction.

"You're barely pregnant, it hardly changed."

"Girl you watch too much TV. There is no such thing as barely pregnant. Either you are or you're not and I am."

Jillian felt flutters in her own stomach, "what do you think Jarvis is going to say?"

"I don't know, there's only one way to find out," she grabbed her purse.

"Can I come?" Jillian looked hopeful.

"No, I'll be back in an hour, tell Grandma Dean I went out."

"I love you Lilly," Jillian called out.

"I love you too Jillybean, it's going to be alright."

Lillian told her sister everything was going to be alright, but she wasn't sure of that herself. As she approached her boyfriend's apartment she was terrified. Jarvis Davis was the star football player at Southwest Florida University, and although he'd only played his freshman year he'd won the starting quarterback position and was a definite meal ticket. Being with him gave her respect. Still the running joke about their relationship was that she would get pregnant and trap him, although it was never her intention.

She used the key he had given her and unlocked the door, "Jarvis are you home?"

"Yeah, I'm in the room," he called out.

She walked in and saw him in his favorite position on the floor with his back against the foot of his bed playing a video game, "hey."

"What's up baby?" His eyes were dead set on the screen.

"We need to talk," Lillian sat on the floor beside him and leaned her back against his bed.

"Talk," he stated flatly still into his game.

"Turn off the game," she demanded.

"Nah girl, I'm in the fourth quarter."

"Damn you!" She stood and turned off the TV.

"What the hell, I'm winning Lillian, what's your problem?"

"I said we need to talk," she stared at him with her hands on her hips.

"After the game," he picked up the remote on the bed and turned the television back on.

"Now!" She hollered with so much authority it made Jarvis jump.

"Fine what?" He tossed the stick on the bed after pausing his game.

"I'm pregnant," she exhaled.

"Say what now?" She suddenly had his undivided attention.

"You heard me," she leaned forward and punched him on the arm.

"Damn," Jarvis shook his head. "My mom warned me about you."

"What's that supposed to mean?"

"I'm a college football player Lillian. I had a tight first season and next year I plan to dominate the field as starting quarterback. My momma told me you were going to try to trap me."

"I can't believe you just said that," Lillian shook her head in disbelief. The thought that he might accuse her crossed her mind, but to hear him make it a reality hurt.

"Are you sure it's mine?" He had the nerve to ask after all the times she'd turned her head the other way when he did his dirt.

She stormed out of the room towards the door.

"Lillian wait, wait, wait," he grabbed her as she entered the hallway. "I'm sorry that was out of line. I didn't mean it."

"Yes you did," she pulled away from him and turned to face him.

"We'll take care of it alright. Come here," he embraced her.

"I'm scared," she finally admitted aloud as she returned his tight hold.

"Don't be," he rubbed her back gently. "First trimester abortions are safer than labor and delivery."

She jerked away from him, "no Jarvis!"

"What do you mean no? We don't have a choice Lillian! You just graduated from high school a few weeks ago, and things are going good for me. We have plenty of time to have kids, but now is not the time."

"You don't have a choice, but I do. I'm having this baby."

"You're emotional and you're not thinking. If it's the money you're worried about, don't. My dad can have the money to me tonight. I'll go with you and everything," he seemed calm as though he'd already suspected that this would happen.

"Fine," she sighed in defeat. "Call him and I'll come by and pick it up tonight."

"Just like that no argument?" He looked surprised. Lillian was not one to bite her tongue. She had no trouble ripping someone to shreds with her tongue.

"I'm tired, and I love you. If you don't want this baby then I won't force you to be a father before you're ready."

He let out a sigh of relief, "I love you Lillian. It's going to be alright."

"I know it is," she smiled. "Listen call me and I'll be back tonight."

"Alright," he kissed her on the cheek. "Don't worry I got this under control."

"I sure do hope so," she sighed. "Don't forget to call me."

Lillian walked back into her bedroom and began to pack her bags and Jillian knew exactly what she was thinking, "Jillybean you know I love you right?"

"Yeah, and we can do this without him," she knew her sister had made up her mind and there was no stopping her.

"No! You have to stay here with Grandma Dean, you have one more year of high school, and I'm not going to let you ruin your life because I did something stupid."

"When will you be back?"

"I don't know," she shrugged. "Maybe never, but I promise I'll contact you eventually."

"What do I tell Grandma Dean?" Jillian began to help her sister pack.

"The truth, she'll understand."

Once Lillian's bags were packed Jillian helped her sister pack her car and they hugged, "I love you Lilly."

"Then take care of yourself. Make me proud," Lillian kissed her sister before getting into her car.

Minutes later she dialed on her phone, "hey Jarvis."

"Hey Lillian I was just about to call you, my dad just left."

He was lying, she could hear the football commentary from his video game in the background, "I'm on my way."

"Alright see you in a minute," he hung up without a bye or an I love you.

Lillian walked up to his apartment and opened the door, "Jarvis?"

"Hey beautiful," he walked up to her and took her hands. "Come in and sit with me."

"I can't stay long," she said as she went and sat in the living room.

"I got you something," he handed her a tiny gift box.

"What is it?" She eyed him suspiciously.

"Open it and see," he grinned.

She opened the case and found a beautiful diamond tennis bracelet inside, "it's gorgeous."

"You're gorgeous," he leaned over and kissed her before sitting beside her on the sofa.

"What did your dad say?" She wanted to know.

"He gave me this," he picked up an envelope off of the coffee table and handed it to her.

"How much?"

"Two-thousand dollars. We figured you'd be feeling down afterwards, so I can take you shopping."

"Thank you," she gave him a half-hearted smile.

He placed his hand firmly against her belly, "I want you to take another test just in case. It's in the bathroom."

She should have known he didn't believe her, "fine."

"It's not that I don't trust you, it's just a possibility that you got a bad test."

"Whatever," Lillian went and locked herself in the bathroom. She took the test again and when the result popped up returned to the living room and threw it at Jarvis in hopes that the applicator would poke his eye out.

He made sure he got a good look at it before he stood, "Lillian I love you. I'm sorry you have to go through this, but I'm going to be there for you."

"I don't want you there. I'm catching a bus out tonight, and I'll be back after it's done."

"Don't you want me to go with you?"

"No! Did you hear what I just said? I don't want you there!"

"Why not?"

"I just want to do it on my own."

"Fine," he was as nonchalant as could be.

"I have to get to the bus station."

"Why?"

"I'm going out of town to get it done. Do you know what kind of drama would be stirred up if someone from church told Grandma Dean what I am doing?"

"You're right," he agreed. "I don't want people to know about this either."

"I'll call you when I get there."

"Are you sure you can't stay for a couple of hours?" He placed his hands on her shoulders and kissed her on the cheek.

"Jarvis you are sick in your head if you think I'm going to get in bed with you," she shook his hands off of her.

"Alright," he looked disappointed. "I love you Lillian."

"It shows," she stated sarcastically with a smile and headed out the door.

Lillian sat in her car and cried until she had no tears left to cry. She cranked up the ignition of her Hyundai Elantra, put it in reverse, then she shifted into first gear, and drove towards her new life.

Jillian had been crying for hours when she heard her grandmother knock on her bedroom door, "ma'am?"

Grandma Dean opened the door, "Jillian where's your sister?"

"Gone," Jillian stated emotionless.

"I thought so," she sighed. "You can't make folks stay where they don't want to be."

"So you knew?"

"Of course, she been eating like a pig and coming home all hours of the night. That Jarvis is just like his daddy. A manwhore."

"Do you know he asked her to have an abortion?"

"But she won't. I raised her better than that, and she's going to be fine."

"I want to crack his skull," Jillian stood and began to pace.

"Let God handle him child, it ain't your place."

"Grandma Dean, is it alright if I go out for a little bit? I can't just sit in here all night."

"Don't stay out too late, we got church tomorrow," she shook her head.

"Yes ma'am," Jillian rushed out the door.

Jillian was a ball of fire as she stormed the streets in search of Jarvis.

"Hey Jillian," Sheldon grabbed her hand. "What are you doing out at this hour?"

She spotted Jarvis. "I'll be back," she marched across the street and pushed her way through the crowd until she was face to face with him.

"What's up Jillian?" He smiled at her.

She slapped him with the might of ten men and he grabbed his face, "you think this is over? It's not! My sister is not just going to abort that baby because you're not man enough to accept the fact that you knocked her up!"

"Your sister loves me, she'll do whatever I say," he said as he caressed his cheek.

Jillian punched him in the chest, "this ain't over. Lillian will be back, so you better get ready because you're that baby's father and there's nothing you can do about it!"

"If you hit me one more time I promise you—"

"You touch her and you won't live to be a father. That's my word!" Sheldon pulled Jillian back and stepped in front of her.

"Hey get her out of here, the quiet ones are always the crazy ones," Jarvis dismissed her with a laugh.

"Jillian come on," Sheldon pulled her hands. "He's not even worth all this."

Jillian turned to Sheldon, "he's going to pay for this."

"Come on Jilly," he pulled her and she followed his lead. "Let's go to my house and talk."

"Okay," she whispered.

Chapter One

"Nicolette Lillian Cotter," Lillian folded the paperwork for her new social security card and stuck it in her purse. She would never be Lillian Hope Carter again. She walked away from that life three weeks before and had no intention of turning back. Now she could use her new name to find a job and finally get on with her life. She managed to find a comfortable one bedroom studio apartment with the money from her ex-boyfriend Jarvis, a decent church, and thus far her car was in working order. The next thing on her agenda would be to find a job, but that would start in the morning.

She walked out into the humid summer heat and headed to her car. One thing her Grandma Dean had taught her was that God had all the answers, and lost and all alone, she was ready to put that ideology to the test. She found Riverside Missionary Baptist Church, a decent sized church unlike the one she grew up in where she could be nothing more than an unnoticed number. It had a congregation of two-thousand plus and seemed to be rapidly growing. Pastor Darius Wright seemed to be an awesome man of God, and she felt like it was home the first time she stepped through the massive cherry wood doors.

During her drive to Wednesday night service she allowed her mind to wander, and she wondered how Jillian was doing. She worried about her sister. Their father had died before they were five and their mother dropped them off at their grandmother's and disappeared without a trace when she was seven. She had always been like a mother to Jillian, although she was only a year older than her, and sheltered her from the real world. Now that she was gone, who did Jillian have to look out for her?

She shook the thought from her mind, her sister would be fine. She would pray her through everything she couldn't see her through, just like Grandma Dean had done for her.

After another excellent sermon Nicolette smiled, it felt good to feel like she belonged. She looked up and caught one of the deacons smiling at her. She didn't know who he was or why he was looking at her, but she wished he would stop. He smiled at her every time she looked his way, and had even waved at her a time or two. Wasn't he there to hear the word of God just like she was?

Nicolette shrugged and bowed her head as Pastor Wright said a closing prayer. She prayed for Jillian, and when Amen rang through the church she stood. She headed for the exit and the happy go lucky deacon tapped her on the shoulder as she was about to walk out of the church.

She whirled around, "what?"

"Good evening," he was grinning from ear to ear. She eyed him and gave him a quick rundown: early twenties, no wedding ring, well groomed, and dressed to impress.

"I'm not from here, so no you don't know me from anywhere," she still had her spitfire attitude.

"I know, but I would like to get to know you. If that's okay with you of course. I noticed you aren't wearing a ring on your finger," he was the typical tall, dark, and handsome.

"How about you give me your name?"

"Darian Wright," he offered his hand and they shook.

"Nicolette Cotter," she eyed him suspiciously. "Is Wright a coincidence or are you a PK?"

"Not all preacher's kids live up to the stereotypes set before them."

"And you're one of those exceptions to the rule I assume?"

"Of course. I love the Lord."

"So are you a deacon?"

"No, but I am the head of the church legal council. I'm in school so I work at the church every Tuesday and Thursday."

"What's the deal bro? Hey miss I'm Adrian, the more attractive of the two Wright brothers as you can see," Adrian Wright smiled at Darian.

"Well what I was about to say before I was so rudely interrupted Darian is that I'm pregnant."

"Pregnant?" Darian's eyes got big.

"Yes Darian two months, don't look so surprised you knew it was bound to happen the way we were going at it," Nicolette kept a straight face.

"But I…" he looked to his brother for help.

"Hey momma, we need a clean up on aisle two, baby momma drama," Adrian called across the church to the pastor's wife.

"Oh God," Darian dropped his head. He focused on the warmth of the mystic sea colored carpet beneath his feet.

Mrs. Wright stormed across the walkway to where Darian was trying not to cry and Adrian was trying not to laugh, "what did you just say?"

"It was a joke momma," Darian never looked up as he spoke.

"Get your narrow behinds in that office now," she pointed and both of them walked off.

Nicolette turned to walk away, "excuse me."

"You too, in the pastor's office," she took Nicolette's hand and led her down the hallway. On Nicolette's first visit to the church the off white walls that were glossed to perfection, and offset by photographs of high ranking church officials, seemed so warm and inviting. Now they held stares of intimidation as Nicolette headed down the never-ending hallway.

Once they were behind closed doors the young men stood on either side of their father who was sitting at his desk. The office was simple compared to the rest of the church. The desk was light oak which contrasted the strength in the dark wood of the pews and other furniture inside of the sanctuary. The ceiling was about ten feet high, a great difference from the vaulted ceiling in the sanctuary which seemed to reach for Heaven. "What's going on?" Pastor Wright asked.

"She just told Darian that she's pregnant," Adrian pointed at Nicolette.

"It was a joke," Darian protested.

"Well it wasn't funny," Pastor Wright spoke out.

"Actually I am pregnant," Nicolette mumbled. "But it happened before I came here, I've only been living here for a few weeks."

"Thank the Lord," Pastor Wright sighed.

"What's your name child?" Mrs. Wright demanded. Her all black dress drifted in a way that was frightening. Her stance showed that she was not one to be messed with without great consequences to follow.

"Lil-I mean Nicolette," she stammered.

"How old are you?"

"Eighteen," she exhaled. "I'm sorry I didn't mean to cause any trouble."

"You didn't cause any trouble at all. Adrian was the one hollering family business across the church like it was a breaking news report."

All eyes were on Adrian, "hey I just heard Darian and baby."

"You know better boy, what is your problem?" Pastor Wright scolded his son.

"Can you come by the church tomorrow morning?" Mrs. Wright asked.

"Actually I have to go out job searching tomorrow."

"If you can be here at nine o'clock tomorrow morning, my son Adrian can help you with that."

"Okay," she shook her head willing to agree to anything that would get her out of that office.

"Then I'll see you tomorrow."

Nicolette turned and headed out of the office. She walked down the hall and sighed, "thank you God."

"Nicolette," Darian jogged to catch up with her. "I'm sorry about my brother."

"No problem," she continued on her path. She entered the foyer and the ambient light from the crystal chandeliers was heavenly. The natural luster it gave the room made her feel soothed, as though the church had been built exclusively for her.

"Here let me get the door for you," he opened the door and she walked outside with him right behind her.

"Thank you," she walked towards her car in the almost empty parking lot.

"Do you mind if I call you sometime?"

"I'm pregnant Darian," she huffed.

"As far as I know pregnancy doesn't affect your ability to speak."

"No I'm not going to sleep with you so go away," she unlocked her car.

"I told you inside I'm a man of God. A good man of God knows a good woman of God when he sees one."

"I just got pregnant a couple of months ago without a husband," Nicolette rolled her eyes.

"And you haven't missed a service, Sunday school, or bible study since you've been coming here," he spoke with pride.

"What are you a secret agent?"

"No, but God makes no mistakes. I think you're here for a reason."

"Goodnight Darian," Nicolette smiled.

"Goodnight, think about what I said now," he opened her car door and allowed her to get in.

She responded with a smile and he shut her door.

Chapter Two

When Nicolette arrived at the church the next morning Darian was sitting outside waiting for her. She decided to be friendly although she expected nothing more than judgment to be passed on her since he now knew she was with child, "good morning Darian."

"Hi Nicolette, how are you this morning?" He beamed.

"Call me Nikki, and are you always so happy?"

"I try," he shrugged.

"We're both adults here let's be serious, what do you want from me?"

"I was worried about you. My family can get pretty theatrical at times and I thought maybe they scared you away last night. I didn't even have your phone number to call you and make sure that you made it home safe," his smile remained bright.

"Well as you can see I'm still all in one piece."

"Yes ma'am," he stared at her as though he were in a trance.

"What?"

"Where are you from?"

"Let's just say southern Florida and leave it at that," she huffed with finality.

"Where is the baby's father?"

"That's none of your business!"

"Sorry," he put his hands up in a defensive gesture. "I did not mean to offend, I was just wondering if he might show up later."

"As far as he knows I went to have an abortion and decided not to come back."

"I'm sorry to hear that," his smile faded a bit.

"Don't be. I'm sure his football games helped him get over his sorrow."

"It's his loss," Darian took her hand and led her into the church. They walked down the hall hand in hand and stopped at the pastor's office. "Knock, knock," Darian called to his parents.

Mrs. Wright did a double take as Pastor Wright smiled and greeted Nicolette by removing her hand from Darian's grip and giving it a firm shake, "good morning young lady."

"Good morning," Nicolette spoke softly.

"Nicolette do you have a resume?" Mrs. Wright cut in.

"No ma'am, I didn't bring a copy with me when I moved."

"That's fine," she smiled. "I'll have my son Adrian work on it with you."

"But I always—" the look Mrs. Wright gave Darian caused him to stop mid-sentence.

"He'll be here shortly, in the mean time have a seat and make yourself comfortable."

"Here," Darian pulled out one of the chairs in front of his father's desk and gestured for her to sit, then he took a seat in the chair beside her.

"Darian don't you have some work you need to be doing in your office?" His mother asked.

"Not really," he shrugged.

"I'm sure you can find something," she glared at him.

"Oh actually there is one thing, come on Nikki, I'll help you get started on that resume until Adrian gets here," he pulled her hand but she resisted.

Nicolette looked over at Mrs. Wright for permission.

"Alright," she exhaled reluctantly.

Darian walked her a few doors down to his office and turned on the light, "excuse the mess. Have a seat in my chair and we'll get started."

"I didn't want to seem rude, but I really don't need help," she stated as she took a seat in the cherry wood desk chair with sand colored upholstered cushions and a matching backrest, which harmonized with the color scheme of the rest of the church.

"Fine," he placed his hands on her shoulders as she began to type.

"I came to this church because it's so big I thought that no one would notice me."

"Well I noticed," he began to massage her shoulders. "And quite a few guys around here have been asking about you."

"I don't like to be the center of attention," it was a lie if she'd ever told one in her life. But she'd made the decision that

Lillian was the life of the party, and Nicolette would remain in a quiet corner.

"And why is that Lillian Carter?"

"What did you just call me?" She got instant chills.

"That is your real name isn't it?" He continued to massage her shoulders.

"How'd you find out?"

"You almost introduced yourself to my parents as Lillian last night, and you just typed it at the top of your resume."

"Oh," she felt sick. "Can you please move your hands that's really distracting."

"Sure," he sighed. "So why did you lie about your name?"

"I didn't. I just changed it a few weeks ago, I have the paperwork in my car to prove it."

"I believe you."

"Is everything going alright in here?" Pastor Wright asked although it was apparent that the first lady had sent him in to check on things as she entered the office on his heels.

"Going great, she types at least sixty-five to seventy words a minute. We need a new secretary maybe we should hire her."

"I don't think so," Nicolette shook her head.

"Why not?" Pastor Wright asked and the first lady elbowed him.

"I don't think you want to portray the image of a pregnant unwed woman as your church secretary."

"She's right," the first lady quickly agreed.

"All have sinned," Darian chimed in and his mother cut her eyes at him.

"Darian I need to speak with you," she spat.

"About what?" He smiled adoringly at her.

"In your father's office," she stormed out of the room and he followed.

"You better watch out there," Pastor Wright grinned. "Darian has quite a crush on you."

"Your wife hates me," she sighed.

"No, not at all. She's just worried that you'll snatch up one of her baby boys. In my eyes they are grown and can do as they wish, but she doesn't see it that way."

"I told him I'm pregnant, I don't understand why he's still attracted to me."

"Sometimes God has a way of showing a man something that no one else can see. I know what Darian's been praying for, and I think it's a very good possibility that he may have found it."

"I don't know about that," Nicolette shrugged. She wasn't quite sure she believed in happily ever after stories.

"Neither do I, but God does," he smiled before exiting the office.

Darian reappeared and placed a sheet of paper on top of the keyboard in front of Nicolette, "fill this out for me and I'll give it to Pastor Wright."

"What is it?"

"An application for the secretary position," he whispered.

"I can't Darian," she frowned.

"Don't make me beg Nikki. You could do a lot of good in this place."

"You don't know me," she sighed.

"But God knows you and it's His will to see you do good things. No one here has the authority to pass judgment on the things you've done."

"Just because they don't have the authority to do so doesn't mean that they won't."

"So let them, God will deal with them. I have a feeling Pastor wants you here as much as I do," he winked.

"What the deal Nicolette?" Adrian came into the room all smiles.

"Good morning," she stared at him.

"I was told that my services were needed."

"Actually we're all done here so you can go," Darian pointed to the door for emphasis.

Nicolette began to fill out the application as the brothers bickered back and forth.

"Don't be like that bro," Adrian grinned.

"What you did last night was messed up," Darian stepped in front of him.

"It was funny," Adrian chuckled.

"Shhh," Nicolette shushed them as she continued to write.

They both stopped and stared at her.

"Nikki can I take you to lunch today?" Darian broke the silence.

"No," she stated flatly and continued to scribble.

"That's cold. She pregnant and she still don't want you," Adrian began to laugh loudly.

Darian stormed out of the office leaving Adrian behind.

"Hey will you go to lunch with me Nicolette?" Adrian stopped hooting long enough to ask.

"No," she continued to write.

"What are you working on?"

"A job application," she responded.

"Put me down as a reference, I'll make sure you get the job."

"No thanks," she sighed.

"Why not?" He caressed her cheek.

"I'm done," she flipped the paper over just as Darian returned with Pastor Wright.

"Young lady is my son pestering you?" Pastor Wright smiled brightly.

"Which one?" She looked at Darian and he quickly averted his eyes.

"Feel free to knock either one of these knuckleheads out," he nudged Darian with his elbow.

"Are you done with the application?" Darian asked still not making eye contact with Nicolette.

"Yes," she extended it in his direction.

"So what do you think is she qualified?" Pastor Wright asked his son.

"Absolutely," Darian responded handing the application to his father.

"Congratulations Miss Cotter, welcome to Riverside Missionary Baptist Church," he folded the application in half without even glancing at it.

"Huh?" Adrian and Nicolette both uttered.

"If Darian recommends you then I don't even have to ask. Now had Adrian been your reference I would be checking you out from now until this time next year," he chuckled.

"What about your wife?" Nicolette wanted to know.

"What about her? I've made a hiring decision, she'll respect that."

"I'm telling momma!" Adrian shook his head.

"Boy go clean the bathrooms," Pastor Wright patted his son on the shoulder. "I heard about what you got into last night."

Adrian shot his brother a how-could-you look and Darian shrugged innocently. "That's foul bro," Adrian grumbled.

"Welcome to Riverside, Miss Cotter," Darian grinned.

Chapter Three

A month passed after Nicolette was hired at Riverside Missionary Baptist Church and the adjustment was a much smoother transition than she had anticipated. She fell right into place and felt at home. Instead of being the church secretary she quickly became the first lady's sidekick. They were even on a first name basis per request of the first lady, which created envy from many long time members.

"Good morning Evelyn," Nicolette peeped into the pastor's office where Mrs. Wright was seated at the pastor's desk.

"Hi Nikki come on in," she was intently staring at the computer screen in front of her. "I need you to put together a few rough draft flyers for me."

"Yes ma'am," Nicolette staggered into the office.

"We have a Fall Family Fun Festival in October," she looked up at Nicolette. "Are you alright?"

"Fine," Nicolette shrugged as she leaned on the desk for support. She'd been feeling dizzy for two days and this morning it was at its worst.

"You don't look too good, have a seat," she pointed to a chair across from where she sat.

"Hey Nikki," Darian walked into the office. He looked at his mother's panicked expression and then to Nicolette, "are you alright?"

"I'm fine really," she'd never fainted before, but she was pretty sure this was how people felt before they passed out.

"Darian get her some water," Evelyn ordered.

"Yes ma'am," Darian disappeared down the hall.

"How do you feel child?" Evelyn stood and walked around the desk planting her hand on Nicolette's forehead.

"I feel alright," Nicolette felt like the room was spinning.

"Don't lie to me. You're in a church."

"Maybe a little dizzy," it was a huge understatement.

"What did you have for breakfast?"

"I don't eat breakfast," she sighed.

"Maybe you don't but that baby needs to eat," she huffed removing her hand from Nicolette and placing it on her hip.

Nicolette rolled her eyes. She hated being told what to do, "I told you I'm fine."

"And I told you not to lie in church, I'm sending you home."

Darian returned with a bottle of water and Pastor Wright at his heels, "here."

"What took you so long?" Evelyn snapped as she opened the bottle. "Drink it."

Nicolette did as she was told then attempted to stand.

"Sit down!" The Wrights shouted in unison, and she flopped back into the chair.

"Where's Adrian?" Evelyn demanded to know.

"Late as usual," Darian shook his head.

She stared at Darian for a moment, "take her home, and make sure she eats something."

"No, I can work really," she assured them although her body told her otherwise.

"Here let me help you young lady," Pastor Wright helped Nicolette to her feet.

Darian took Nicolette's hand and made her focus shift from her giddiness to his gentle touch, "let's go."

"But I'm fine," she whimpered.

He ignored her and she followed his lead reluctantly. She knew he'd been trying to get alone with her for weeks, and they were making it too easy for him, "just relax, I've got everything under control."

"That's exactly what I'm afraid of," she mumbled.

Nicolette decided to use her dizzy spell to her advantage and kept her eyes shut for almost the entire drive home.

"We're here," Darian sang as he pulled up in front of her apartment.

"Thanks, I'll see you tomorrow," she reached to unbuckle her seatbelt and he placed his hand on top of hers.

"I have to make sure you're settled in and that you get something to eat first," he removed his hand from hers and turned off the ignition.

"I think I can manage," she tried to be friendly.

"No, you don't understand. When Evelyn Wright instructs you to do something you don't have a choice in the matter," he smiled. "Besides I'd like to see where you live."

She closed her eyes, "you can't."

"Why not?"

"I'd just rather you didn't."

"Come on Nikki it can't be that bad, you've seen my office, I'm not the neatest person either."

"It's organized, I just don't have much," she sighed.

"I don't care about that," it was clear he was not going to give up.

"Fine, but don't say I didn't warn you," she got out of the car and he joined her in front of the apartment. She opened the door, "come in."

He stepped inside closing the door behind him, "hold on a minute." He whipped out his cell phone and began to push buttons on it, "hey dad."

"What are you doing?" She didn't like the look he was giving her.

"We just got to Nikki's apartment," he listened for a while. "She doesn't even have a bed."

"I do too!" Nicolette protested pointing to the air mattress on the floor.

"She needs furniture," he sighed.

"See this is why I didn't want you to come in here, I don't need anything!" She was irritated.

"Okay, I'll let her know," he hung up the phone.

"Why did you do that?"

"Do what?"

"I don't need anything."

"Nikki you sleep on the floor."

"I sleep on a mattress."

"You're three months pregnant, what's going to happen a few months from now when you get down there to go to bed and can't get up in the morning?"

"I can take care of myself I've been doing it for years," she glared at him.

"I want to help you," he tried to take her hand and she backed away.

"I don't want your help!"

"Nikki I care for you a lot, and my parents adore you. I want you to be able to come to me when you need something," the sincerity in his voice caught her off guard. She had dealt with enough careless people to know the difference, and it seemed that he really was concerned.

"I appreciate that, but I don't need anything," she shook her head adamantly.

He grabbed her hand, "how do you feel?"

"Fine," she forced herself to smile.

"You look like you feel better. I think my mom has been stressing you out, she's good at that," he chuckled.

"She's growing on me."

"I love you Nikki," she wasn't sure if he realized what he'd said to her.

"But you don't know me."

"I want you to be happy, and I want you to be well taken care of."

"I can take care of myself."

"I know, but you don't have to."

"I don't get it," she shook her head in confusion.

"Get what?"

"What do you want from me?"

"I want to get to know you. I want to know what makes you cry, so I can be the one to always make you smile."

"Aren't those the words to a *Joe* song?"

"Maybe so, but maybe he said it best. Nikki I don't know why God does some things, but I don't believe you were put in my life to just be a stranger passing through."

"Now that's surprising," she sighed.

"What? That I'm not trying to get in bed with you?"

"No, that Darian Wright listens to secular music."

They both laughed, and their laughter was followed by an awkward moment of silence.

"You really should smile more often. You're very pretty," his closeness made her undeniably uncomfortable.

"Thank you," she pulled her hand from his grip and walked into the kitchen. "Can I get you something?"

"No thanks, but I want you to eat something. If you don't I'll have to tell my mom on you, then I'll get in trouble," he poked out his bottom lip and gave her his most pitiful look.

"Evelyn Wright is no push over that's for sure."

"Hold on a sec," he responded to his vibrating cell phone. "Yes ma'am?...I'm trying to get her to eat something...I know Ma...she looks like she feels better...I heard you," he rolled his eyes. "No ma'am...yes ma'am...hold on," he extended the phone in Nicolette's direction.

"Hello?" Nicolette spoke into the phone.

"Why haven't you eaten, Darian should have taken you somewhere."

"I'm fine Evelyn," she sighed.

"You're not fine, you're pregnant and you're starving an innocent child, and don't you dare roll your eyes," she hissed just as Nicolette was on the verge of doing it. Darian caught on and laughed.

"I'll get something in a minute."

"You'll get something now is that understood?"

"Yes ma'am," Nicolette rolled her eyes.

"Didn't I just tell you not to roll your eyes?"

"I...yes ma'am."

"What's this I hear about you sleeping on the floor?"

"I have a bed."

"It's an air mattress!" Darian called out.

"An air mattress? Child what happens a few months from now when you go to bed and can't get up off of that floor in the morning?" Evelyn hollered through the phone.

"That's what I told her," Darian called.

"Shut up Darian!" Evelyn belted out causing Nicolette to move the phone from her ear. "And make her something to eat!"

"Evelyn I have been taking care of myself for years," Nicolette informed her.

"That's apparent," she spat. "You may be young now, but the damage you're doing is going to last a lifetime. If you'd had someone to take care of you maybe you would be more educated concerning these things."

Nicolette took that as an insult to her grandmother, "wait a minute!"

"Nikki shhhh," Darian pleaded.

"My grandmother did the best she could, and I'm not about to let you negate that."

"I'm sure she did," Evelyn's tone was softer.

"She is a very old woman, she could only do so much at her age."

"Nikki," Darian forced her to look at him. "Shhh."

"Let me speak to Darian," Evelyn huffed.

"Here," Nicolette handed Darian the phone and walked off. She went into the bathroom and fought the urge to shed tears. She would not allow Evelyn Wright to downsize what Grandma Dean had done for her. Her grandmother had given birth to her mother at the age of forty-five and became a mother again in her sixties when her mother had abandoned her and her little sister Jillian. As far as Nicolette was concerned no one could have done a better job at raising her. Nicolette knew that her mistakes were her own and no fault of Grandma Dean.

"Nikki are you alright in there?" Darian knocked on the door.

"Leave me alone!"

"Nikki please open the door, my parents are on their way over here."

She opened the door and glared at him, "why did you call them?"

"Because I want to make sure that you're taken care of," he reached out and gently stroked her hair. "My family is dramatic at times, but we all care about those around us. I want to help you in any way that I can."

"I told you I don't need help," she protested. "I can take care of myself."

"I know you can, but you don't have to. Nikki let me be there for you and this child. If as nothing more then at least as your friend."

"Why is it that men think that pregnant women and women with kids are desperate?"

"Ouch," he looked down. "Am I that bad that a woman has to be desperate to want me?"

"No, but you think because your father is the pastor you're all that and all of the women in the church want you. I have news for you Darian Wright, I don't want you!"

"I apologize Nikki. I didn't know you felt that way," he turned away from her, but she knew she'd hurt his feelings. "Let's just wait for my parents to get here."

"Darian?" She exhaled.

"Yes," he kept his back to her.

"I'm sorry," she sighed.

"It's okay," he huffed. "We can't help how we feel right?"

"Turn around and look at me," she demanded.

He turned around.

"I am attracted to you," she admitted. "I just don't understand why you would want anything to do with me."

"Why wouldn't I?" His eyes begged her to see what he saw.

She took his hand and placed it on her stomach, "because this is not going anywhere."

"I think I'd make a good father. My son would agree."

Shock registered on her face and she took a step away from him, "oh."

"Well not necessarily a father, maybe a father figure or role model," he shrugged. "Midnight my Chihuahua is my son by the way."

She smiled at him, "I know you will be a good father one day. You're a great guy. I wish I'd met you before all this happened."

"God makes no mistakes, this is a faithful servant of the Lord," he pointed to her soon to be bulging belly.

"I know," she nodded in agreement. "But our meeting is just bad timing."

Darian chuckled, "girl God is always right on time."

There was another silence between the two and this time both of them were very comfortable, "so why do you think God put us here today?"

He tilted her chin and looked down into her eyes, "I think it's up to us to figure that out."

Before they had a chance to figure it out the doorbell rang, "must be your people, I don't know anyone here."

"There's no way they got here that fast," he turned away from her.

"You said it yourself, God is always on time. Maybe something that we didn't need to happen between us was about to happen."

Darian turned back to her, "God knows I don't give up that easily." He headed for the door and let his parents in.

"What took you so long to answer the door?" Evelyn barked when he opened the door as she pushed her way in.

"Ma?" Darian called behind his mother.

"Nikki how in the world do you get up off of this floor in the morning? I'm not even pregnant and I can't get up from something that low on the ground."

"She's eighteen years old," Pastor Wright responded. "When you were young you would have been fine down there too."

Evelyn shot him a who-asked-you look and she turned away, "Nikki?"

"What?" Nicolette barked and Darian and Pastor Wright gasped in response.

"I'm sorry Nikki," Evelyn apologized and Darian and his father gasped again. "I know I offended you when I mentioned your upbringing, but it was unintentional. I'm sure your grandmother did a great job of raising you and it shows. You're well mannered and fairly responsible for your age."

"I can take care of myself," Nicolette fought the urge to shed tears.

"You have to know that I care about you, I've never had a daughter before and I'm concerned about you."

"I don't want any help," Nicolette whispered. "I want to do it all on my own."

Evelyn embraced her, "child if any of us could do it alone God wouldn't bring us together. You are a part of my administrative staff, your need is my need."

A phone began to ring and Pastor Wright answered, "hello?"

"Hey dad where is everyone?" It was Adrian Wright on speakerphone.

"Where are you?"

"At the church," he sighed.

"Boy you're an hour late!" High strung Evelyn Wright had returned as she released Nicolette. "Clean up your brother's office and make sure you read the notes I left for you on your father's desk."

"Yes ma'am," Adrian responded dully.

"We'll call you," Pastor Wright said before hanging up.

Evelyn whisked into the kitchen and began searching the cabinets like a mad woman, "we may as well go to the house."

"Nikki I'd love it if you'd join us at our home for the day," Pastor Wright grinned at her.

"I can't," Nicolette looked at Darian whose eyes were pleading with her.

"Darian won't be around to bother you if that's what you're concerned about," Evelyn looked back and forth between the two. "He has other things to take care of today don't you Darian?"

"Oh yes ma'am," Darian nodded in confused agreement.

After spending a day with the pastor and first lady of RMBC, Nicolette was counting her blessings. They were good people and she felt blessed to be in their presence. She had seen a new side of Evelyn, a loving compassionate side. There was no doubt about the genuineness of the love shared between Mr. and Mrs. Wright.

A few times throughout the day she'd even caught herself wondering if Darian was as sincere as his father. Evelyn had given Adrian and Darian strict instructions on what they were to do, and she had not seen them since. She enjoyed the day which had consisted of being ministered to, talking about raising Adrian and Darian, and led to looking at pictures.

"Hey what's so funny?" Darian asked as he walked up to the dining room table where Evelyn and Nicolette were laughing at Darian's first birthday picture where he had cake and icing everywhere but around his mouth.

"You are," Nicolette smiled in his direction then moved her eyes back to the picture.

"Aw Ma! Not the photo album," he looked distressed.

"Boy hush," Evelyn dismissed him.

"Oh good, you didn't get that far yet," he looked at her and raised his eyebrow.

"Did you two get it all done?"

"I got it all done, Adrian skipped out on me."

"What do you mean he skipped out on you?"

"He left me hanging, talking about he had a date at noon."

"I told him I needed him to take Nikki home tonight."

"I told him to call you," Darian shook his head.

"Nikki do you think you can drive yourself home if Darian takes you to the church to get your car?"

"Yes ma'am," Nicolette shook her head.

"Alright," she shut the photo album with a smile.

"I'll see you in the morning," Nicolette stood with a smile.

"Good," Evelyn gave her a satisfied nod. "Darian tell your brother to call me as soon as you hear from him."

"Yes ma'am," Darian responded as they headed for the door.

"Do you mind if I come in for a minute?" Darian asked when Nicolette got out of her car, which was parked beside his.

"Come on," she shrugged as he followed her to the front door. She opened the door and flipped on the lights, "I should have known you were up to something."

"My momma made me do it. She even stole your keys when you weren't looking," he put his hands up innocently.

The once bare apartment was now fully furnished, "I don't know what to say."

"Do you like it?" They stepped inside and Darian locked the door.

"It's beautiful, but I can't accept all of this. I'm sure there are people in that church who need this more than I do."

"This stuff didn't come from the church. Most of it belonged to my parents, the rest they got for you as a welcome to Riverside gift."

"But I don't need any help," she mumbled.

"We love you Nikki, you're a part of our family now. You don't have to do this on your own."

"What are the people in the church going to think about this?"

"The only ones who know about this are us, my brother, and my parents. It's not anyone else's business."

"Thank you," her voice was barely audible.

"I'm glad you like it because I'm exhausted," he placed his hands on her shoulders and began to gently massage her. Suddenly Nicolette began to bawl and he turned her around and held her in his arms. "Was it something I said?" He wondered aloud. "Nikki whatever it is will be alright I promise you."

"My life is not supposed to turn out this way," she told him between tears.

"I know Nikki, but when things look bad they really may not be," he responded.

"Darian I'm scared," she'd finally admitted a reality she didn't want to face.

"God doesn't want you to go through this alone," he kissed her gently on the forehead and wiped the tears from her cheeks. "Let me go through this with you Nikki."

When Nicolette turned over in her bed the arm around her held her a little tighter, "are you alright?"

She instantly felt sick, "your mother is going to kill me."

"Let me deal with her," he kissed her on the cheek with his arm still wrapped around her.

"Darian you don't understand, earlier today your mother asked me if there was something going on between us, and I looked her in the eyes and told her there wasn't. If she finds out about this she is going to think I set it all up, and never trust me again. My word means a lot to me."

"Shh, Nikki it's alright really."

"No it's not," she finally jerked hard enough to pull away from him and sat up. "Your father likes me, now what will he think of me?"

"Nikki that man knows me better than I know myself. He told me two days ago to stay out of your bed." He chuckled, "I'm sure he already knows exactly where I am right now."

"How can you laugh about this? It's not funny! And why would you do it if your father told you not to?"

"Calm down girl," he sat up and wrapped his arms around her. "You're acting like we did something wrong."

"Hello? We did!"

"Nikki," Darian laughed. "You were upset, and you were crying. You needed someone to hold you and be there for you. The only thing I even took off was my shoes. It's not like anything went on between us."

"Maybe not but I wanted something more to happen," she whispered.

"So did I," he sounded relieved to admit. "I'm not confused about my feelings Nikki, I want to be committed to you. If you would quit being so stubborn we could move on and really get to know each other. I want to take you out, and I want to help you get ready for this baby. As a matter of fact, I want to go to your next doctor's appointment."

"Evelyn's not going to go for this," she bit her lip at the thought of the tongue lashing she was in for.

"Stop worrying about my mom, her bark is worse than her bite."

"Don't even try that lie on me Darian. I've seen her bite and it's lethal, she had your brother in tears the other day."

Darian wrapped his arms tight around Nicolette's waist and pulled her down to the pillow beside him. "Worrying is not good for this baby," he began to rub her belly. "So when's your next doctor's appointment?"

"I haven't made one yet," she sighed.

"Let me know when you make your next one," he sighed.

"I don't have insurance," she looked into his eyes.

"Nikki?" His voice was as calm as his emotions would allow. "Please tell me you haven't just gone through an entire trimester of pregnancy without seeing a doctor."

"You need to go," Nicolette removed his hand from around her and closed her eyes.

"I just asked you a question," he sat up calmly.

"I'll get to the doctor when I can afford to. I don't want to talk about the baby anymore."

"Fine," she felt Darian getting off of the bed. Seconds later he kissed her on the cheek and her eyes remained shut. Footsteps walked across the house followed by the sound of her front door shutting.

Chapter Four

"These announcements look great," Evelyn smiled at Nicolette. "I'm really impressed."

"Thank you," Nicolette gave her a nervous nod. She hadn't seen Darian all morning, and after the night before she felt like she was walking on pens and needles.

"Good morning young lady," Pastor Wright chimed as he entered the office.

"Good morning," she looked in his direction.

"You haven't seen Darian by chance have you? His class was canceled this morning and it's not like him to be late," the way he was staring at her made her want to jump up and run.

"Not since he left my apartment." she sighed.

"About what time was that?" Evelyn asked and Pastor Wright winced as though he'd been punched in the stomach.

"I'll just try to call him again," Pastor Wright pulled out his cell phone. "Darian where are you I've been calling you...Is everything alright?...Okay."

"What did he say?" Evelyn demanded to know.

"He's in the parking lot," Pastor Wright shrugged. "Says he was talking to Adrian."

"Good morning everybody," Adrian was all smiles as he entered the office and the look he gave Nicolette told her he knew something.

"Oh God," Nicolette accidentally spoke out loud at the endless possibilities of lies Darian may have shared with his brother.

"Are you alright?" Mr. and Mrs. Wright asked in unison.

"Excuse me," Nicolette stood up and headed into the hallway.

"Nikki, you alright?" Darian grabbed her arm.

"I'll be back," she pulled away and hurried down the hall to the ladies room.

"Nikki are you sick?" Darian's voice was loud and clear as she locked the stall.

"What are you doing in here?" She asked.

"Darian, what are you doing?" Evelyn took over.

"I just almost got knocked out by Nikki trying to get over here, so I was checking to make sure she was alright."

"Get out!"

"Yes ma'am," Nicolette could hear the door open and shut.

"Nikki are you alright?"

"Yes. I'll be out in a second. I just thought I was going to be sick."

"What did you have for breakfast this morning?"

Her response was silence.

"Come out here," Evelyn knocked on the door.

Nicolette did as she was told, "I'm fine."

"Nikki you have to stop doing this to yourself. I know you've been thinking about yourself for the last eighteen years, but now you have to think about not only yourself, but that baby too."

"I know," Nicolette mumbled as she washed her hands and face.

Evelyn handed her a paper towel, "I'll send Adrian to get you something to eat."

They reentered the office and the foregoing conversation fell silent, but Nicolette had a feeling she was the subject.

"Adrian I need you to go and pick up breakfast for Nikki," Evelyn informed him.

"Then I'm going to need some gas money?" He extended his hand.

"I just gave you money for gas two days ago," Pastor Wright stated.

"I know man. Save yourself some money and send Darian. He won't charge you a dime," Adrian smirked at his brother.

"I asked you to do it, besides Darian has other things to take care of," Evelyn snapped.

"Man this ain't fair, Darian's the one who spent the night with her last night," Adrian grumbled as he headed out the door.

"What did you just say?" Evelyn barked.

"Don't act so surprised Ma, she came through the door with a baby on the way, you knew she was a hoe."

"Adrian!" Pastor Wright hollered.

"I told you, I told you!" Evelyn yelled at her husband. "Now look what's happened!"

"Nothing happened!" Darian called out.

"Shut up!" Evelyn screeched. "The only reason I hired you was so that I could keep an eye on you, I knew you were up to something."

"Excuse me," Nicolette pushed her way through and Darian grabbed her.

"Nikki wait," he sighed.

"Let her go Darian," Evelyn ordered.

"If she goes, then I go with her."

"So you've allowed a woman to cause you to disobey your parents?"

"Just stay Darian, I don't need anyone!" Nicolette snatched away and rushed out to her car. A part of her hoped that Darian would follow, but after crying in her car for a couple of minutes she realized that wish was not going to come true.

Darian had been knocking on Nicolette's door and ringing her doorbell for ten minutes when she finally decided to answer.

"Girl, I've been worried sick about you," he embraced her.

"I told you I didn't need help, if you hadn't called them yesterday none of this would have ever happened!"

"So all of this is my fault?" He leaned on her door until it shut.

"No, I just saw this coming. I tried to save you from it," she shrugged.

"I'm just glad you're alright, I've been sick to my stomach all day thinking something happened after you left."

"Something like what?"

"I don't know," he shrugged. "People do crazy things when they're upset."

"I'm not suicidal if that's what you're getting at."

"Nikki I meant everything I said to you. I want to be with you, and now my whole family knows it," he seemed relieved.

"So what happened after I left?" Nicolette asked as he pulled her hand and led her to the sofa and gestured for her to sit.

"I told my mom to shut up and listen for once in her life," he seemed proud of himself.

Nicolette gave him a look of total disbelief as she took a seat, "you actually said that?"

"I know, I can't believe I lived to tell it, but she was way out of line and so was Adrian and I was pissed off. I don't know if I've ever been so mad with them in my life," he sat beside her.

"How did she react to that?" Nicolette wanted to know.

"She shut up and she listened," he shrugged. "I told her that I want to date you, and if she doesn't like it that is her business."

"I'm not coming between you and your family," Nicolette shook her head.

"You don't have to, my mom knows she was dead wrong for what she said to you, and I promise you she'll apologize to you first thing tomorrow morning when you go to work."

"Are you kidding me?" She shot him a sideways glance, "I'm not going back there."

"Nikki you have to, you work there," Darian reminded her.

"Not anymore, I quit. Besides I can't even look at your mom, I know she thinks we slept together, and once that woman has her mind set on something there is no changing it."

"Nikki I don't lie to my mother. She knows the truth. I followed you home from the church to make sure you made it alright, and when I went inside with you, and you started to cry, I just wanted to hold you, and make you feel like things were alright, even if it was only temporary. You didn't push me away, so I can only assume it was what you wanted me to do. You cried yourself to sleep, and maybe it was wrong of me to stay, but I didn't want to wake you, and I didn't want to leave without telling you. I lost sight of the fact that I was there to comfort you, and began to think about myself. I love you."

"This is insane Darian, are you listening to yourself? I'm carrying another man's baby, and you're telling me you want to hook up with me."

"I don't want to hook up with you, I want to...be committed to you and there is a big difference. I didn't expect this, but I'm not going to pretend that my feelings don't exist because of what people might think. When I held you in my arms last night I felt like I was holding my beautiful pregnant wife."

"Wow," Nicolette shot to her feet as though she'd felt an electric shock. "I don't need a husband. I can make it on my own."

"I didn't get to tell you that the reason I was late for work this morning was because I was on the phone with my insurance company. I added you and the baby."

"You can't do that without my permission," she sighed.

"Well I did," he shrugged.

"Why? I just don't understand why you care so much, and to be honest with you it's frustrating."

"Nikki you said you have feelings for me," he stood beside her.

"I do, but I'm not going to ruin your life."

"I'm twenty years old, I think I'm old enough to make my own decisions don't you? I'm not asking you to tell me you love me, but I want you to know that I love you."

"How do you know that?" She challenged him.

"Every time I see you I can't help but smile. I look forward to every new day because I know I'll get to hear your voice. Nikki last night when you admitted to me that you were afraid, I would have done anything to take all of your fears away. This is it girl, I know it," he caressed her cheek and it gave her chills.

"I don't know about all that," she shook her head.

"You're a faithful servant of the Lord, you've proven that," he gave her a sly smile. "And you believe God's word right?"

"Of course," she nodded.

"I'll be back, I need to get my Bible from the car," he rushed out the front door. Seconds later he returned, "let's sit at the table."

"What are you up to Darian?" She asked him.

"You'll see," he chuckled lightly.

"My grandmother taught me well. I know the Bible, I'll go toe to toe with you if I have to."

"Let's go then," he pulled out a chair for her and then fell into the one beside her.

"Let's look at *Ecclesiastes 4:9*," he flipped in his Bible to a page he'd already marked.

"You're trying to set me up and it's not going to work," Nicolette sang the words.

"No I'm trying to remove that independent woman spell society has cast on you, Miss I Don't Need Anyone."

"Good luck with that one," she rolled her eyes.

"*Two are better than one; because they have a good reward for their labour. For if they fall, the one will lift up his fellow: but woe unto him that is alone when he falleth; for he hath not another to help him up.*" He smiled at her.

Nicolette rolled her eyes, "I am not impressed. I've seen the Life Alert commercials."

"*Again, if two lie together, then they have heat: but how can one be warm alone?* It gets cold here in Georgia, Florida girl," he caressed her cheek and she slapped his hand away.

"I got a heater and a blanket," she stated seriously.

"Girl, come on now! '*And if one prevail against him, two shall withstand him; and a threefold cord is not quickly broken.*'"

Nicolette stared at him for a moment, "say what now?"

"It means—"

"I know what it means, but I can fight boy, I'm from the hood."

"God," he looked to Heaven for help. "Why is she so stubborn?"

The doorbell rang and Nicolette looked at him, "that must be your people."

"Why do you say that?"

"No one knows where I live," Nicolette shrugged.

Darian hopped up and went to get the door, "hey what are you doing here?"

"Where's Nikki?" Evelyn asked as she pushed her way in like she owned the apartment.

Pastor Wright followed with a bouquet of roses in hand, "Good evening young lady, I apologize for us dropping by unannounced."

"You have nothing to apologize about," Nicolette shifted her eyes towards Evelyn.

"You're right, but I do, Nikki I'm sorry. I overreacted a little and I apologize."

"A little?" Darian and Pastor Wright questioned as one voice.

"Nikki I love my sons, but I know they have to live their own lives. You're about to be a mother, then you'll understand why I am so protective over my boys."

"We trust Darian's judgment, and if he thinks this is what God wants for him, then we support him," Pastor Wright handed her the flowers.

Nicolette shook her head, "I can—"

"Take care of myself," Darian finished her sentence in a mocking tone. "But you don't have to."

"What are the two of you up to?" Evelyn asked.

"Bible study," Darian pointed to the open book on the table.

"What are you reading?" Pastor Wright began to read the open page. "Darian?"

"I know," he nodded.

"Good luck with that one, she's a stubborn one," he chuckled.

"What?" Evelyn began to read.

"I could use a little help with this," Darian confirmed.

"What are you trying to do propose to the girl?" Evelyn asked.

"Maybe," he shrugged and Evelyn's mouth dropped open. "But for now I just want to get rid of this I can do it by myself attitude she has."

"Like I said before...good luck," Pastor Wright winked at Nicolette.

"Man this girl got a cell phone if she falls, she got a heater in the cold, and forget about a partner to take on an attacker, she probably has a gun."

"I told you I know the Bible," she shrugged.

"Well then you know Proverbs 18:22 says *'whoso findeth a wife findeth a good thing,'*?"

"Yep and I also know Ephesians 5:24."

"Oh boy," Pastor Wright knew where Darian was headed. "You might want to change the subject right about now son."

"Why?" Darian continued to flip through the New Testament until he came to the verse and read it in silence.

"I'm not cut out to be a submissive wife," she informed them.

"Keep reading son," Pastor Wright touched his son on the back.

As Darian began to read aloud his father spoke along with him, "*Husbands, love your wives, even as Christ also loved the church, and gave himself for it.*"

"If a man loves you he's not going to ask you to submit to anything that's not God's will," Pastor Wright stated.

"This is just too fast for me," Nicolette commented.

"But it will all work out," Darian assured her.

"You can't be serious," Evelyn shook her head.

"Let he without sin cast the first stone," Pastor Wright shot her a challenging look.

Evelyn's response was silence.

"Nikki there's something you should know about me," he looked at his mom with a smile.

"You better not!" Evelyn spoke between gritted teeth.

"The truth shall set you free," Darian and Pastor Wright obviously knew something Evelyn didn't want Nicolette to know.

Chapter Five

"What can I do for you Deacon Turtle?" Pastor Wright asked.

"I'd really rather not discuss it in front of other people," he moved his eyes to Nicolette.

"She's family it's alright, what's on your mind?"

"I thought it'd be best to inform you of what some of the church board members have been discussing behind your back before it hits the fan," he sighed. "A few people want you removed as our church Pastor?"

"What?" Evelyn called out in horror.

"Nelson are you sure?" Pastor Wright wanted to know.

"Positive, they are having a meeting today to discuss it behind your back."

"Well did they give a reason?" Evelyn demanded to know.

"Her," he pointed at Nicolette.

"I told you this was coming Darius but did you want to listen to me? Of course not!" Evelyn scolded her husband like a child.

The office door opened and Adrian appeared all smiles with lipstick on his lips, "hey everybody sorry I'm late. I had to try to break through a crowd of angry demanding women, and another crowd of desperate overfriendly women. With Darian off the market I'm a celebrity now."

"Shut the door," Evelyn sighed. "Please continue Deacon Turtle."

"There are rumors about her being pregnant," he shook his head in disbelief.

"She is, and it's nobody's business but her own," Darian glared at the deacon with fire in his eyes.

"Don't shoot me Darian I'm just the messenger."

"People think that you were aware of her pregnancy when you hired her," once again the deacon shook his head in disbelief.

"I was," Pastor Wright confirmed and the look Evelyn gave him was lethal.

"And is it safe to assume that Darian is the father?"

"Well he is—"

"Yes," Darian spoke out as he balled his fists.

"Was anything else said?"

"No, I'll be able to tell you more after the meeting this afternoon. All I can say is that some want the family removed from their positions at this church. No matter what happens I'm on your side," Deacon Turtle gave a loyal nod.

"I appreciate that Nelson," Pastor Wright said as he watched the deacon excuse himself.

"There's really a simple solution to this," Evelyn said.

"No Ma," Darian protested. "It's none of their business, if they want to talk let them talk."

"We have worked too hard Darian! I am not going to allow this to happen, so I'm sorry, but they need to know the truth."

"You tell my truth and I'll tell yours," he glared at his mother and she looked away. "What's wrong Ma?"

"Darian you are out of line son," Pastor Wright boomed.

"She was out of line when she did what she did. Like mother like son," he huffed.

"Darian stop man this ain't even necessary," Adrian stepped in front of his brother in an attempt to make him focus.

"I can't live my life because I always have to worry about what the church is going to think. I'm sick of it. This place is a damn joke!"

"Darian!" Pastor Wright shouted. "Don't let him win. He's trying to come in and tear this church apart because we are doing good things."

Nicolette decided she'd heard enough and stood, "let me just make this easy for everyone and leave."

"Thank you," Evelyn let out a sigh of relief. "There's a really good church on—"

"Evelyn," Pastor Wright's tone was firm. "She already has a church."

"Then we have to tell everyone the baby is not Darian's. They'll destroy us if we don't. Besides even if we keep this under wraps, they'll all find out when the baby is born and it looks nothing like Darian."

"I'm so sorry," Nicolette whispered with tear-filled eyes.

"Young lady you have nothing to apologize about. Darian take her home, your mother and I will handle this," Pastor Wright spoke with confidence.

"Yes sir," Darian was calmer.

"I just don't understand," Nicolette was dwelling on Deacon Turtle's words hours later.

"Baptists," Darian shook his head. "I am telling you what I know Nikki, they are the meanest bunch of people out there. I've seen churches destroyed by them when they don't like something, pastors stripped of their churches for senseless reasons. They've lost their homes, cars, jobs, and their lives work in a matter of minutes."

"I feel terrible, this is all my fault," she sighed.

"No it's not. People envy my dad's position, it comes with the job. If it wasn't our relationship it would be something else. They'll have to dig a lot deeper than this to uproot the seeds my father has planted into this ministry. We have nothing to worry about."

"You seem so confident."

"I am," he smiled. "But enough about that. I want you to meet someone. Will you come to my apartment with me?"

"And give the church spies something else to talk about?"

"Nikki I had to learn a long time ago that you cannot live your life in fear that someone from the church is going to see you. You'd have to stop living and they still wouldn't be satisfied. As long as what we do is alright with God no one else matters."

"Then let's go."

The tiny black dog came charging towards Nicolette and Darian with a blanket hanging from its mouth.

"There's my man," Darian grinned as he knelt down and scooped up the small dog. "I missed you."

"So this is Midnight?" Nicolette asked.

"Yeah, this is my baby," he smiled with pride yanking the baby blanket from the dog's mouth. "Isn't he adorable?"

Nicolette didn't want to disagree, but she didn't want to lie, "I guess in a furry, drooling, kind of way."

"So you don't like dogs?"

"They don't like me," she shrugged.

"Midnight likes everybody, isn't that right?" Darian cooed.

Nicolette rolled her eyes, "I'm just glad you have a Chihuahua and not a Great Dane or a German Shepherd."

"Don't let the size fool you, he's not going to let anyone push him around," Darian laughed as he put him down. "Go play in your room."

"He has a room?" Nicolette smiled.

"Come on," he pulled her down the hallway.

She looked into the bedroom which had a small toddler bed lined with stuffed animals and dog toys sprawled all over the floor. "Your dog has his own television?" Nicolette nodded towards the set on a small table in the corner.

"He loves Disney movies," Darian smiled at the thought.

She began to laugh, "boy and I thought I was crazy."

"He's really smart," Darian put an arm around Nicolette and Midnight froze and began to bark.

"See he doesn't like me," she shrugged.

"Hush boy, don't you see we have company? Clean up this mess," Darian scolded him.

The dog immediately began to pick up the dog toys scattered over the floor one by one and placed them in his toy box.

Darian walked over to the television and turned it on, "come on he'll just play in here."

"I can't believe your dog has his own room," Nicolette giggled.

"He's my baby, I have to spoil someone," he grinned. "Have a seat, kick off your shoes, and make yourself comfortable."

Nicolette kicked off her shoes and plopped down on the sofa, "I didn't even have my own room until I was eighteen and moved here."

"Same here, I didn't have my own until I was sixteen, Adrian moved out on his own on his eighteenth birthday," Darian took a seat beside her. "Make yourself comfortable baby put your feet up. I cleaned this house for you, so you better relax," he pulled her towards him and she propped her legs up on the arm of the sofa.

"You cleaned up for me?" She looked around the apartment in search of the clean part. There were pens, pencils, and books piled on the coffee table hiding a one inch layer of dust. The corner of the living room held a pile of clothes that was higher than the chair beside it. What Nicolette was sure was once scattered all over the house had now become individual piles of clutter.

"Yeah, I tried anyway why what's wrong with it?"

"Nothing, if you live in a jungle. The dog cleans up better than you do," she teased.

"That's mean," he kissed her on the nape of her neck.

"Darian I love you," Nicolette exhaled the words she'd wanted to say for days and hadn't worked up the nerve to speak though Darian had said them to her many times.

"I love you too girl," Darian held her even tighter. "I could hold you forever."

"What are we going to do if things get ugly at the church?"

"You worry too much, God's got everything under control," he was as nonchalant as could be.

"What if He doesn't?"

"You need to relax girl, have a little faith," he sighed. "One high strung woman in the Wright family is more than enough. My mom is a heart attack waiting to happen."

"You really shouldn't say that about your mother."

"I know, but I have never met anyone else who takes making a mountain out of a mole hill to a whole new level."

"She does take things to the extreme at times, but it's just her personality."

"Don't get me wrong, I love my mom. I just worry about her because she gets stressed out over things that aren't even worth the energy. As much as I love Evelyn Wright, I don't want you to become her. Some days she has you so uptight I feel guilty because I encouraged you to take the job as church secretary."

"I'm a big girl, I can handle it," she assured him.

Darian's phone chimed and he released Nicolette causing her to sit up and stare at him, "hello…Yes sir?…On a Sunday night?…Just tell me when and where and I'll be there…I'll let her know…Yes sir…Bye."

"What?" Was Nicolette's response to the uneasy expression on Darian's face.

"That was my dad, they're having a board meeting tonight to try to vote him out."

"Why so soon?"

"I told you because they're Baptists, it's their way or no way," he shook his head in disbelief. "I have to get down there."

"I understand," she tried to smile.

"My dad said it would mean a lot to him if you'd be there," he gently caressed her shoulder.

"Darian I don't think so," Nicolette shook her head in disagreement.

"I'm sure he'll understand," Darian looked genuinely disappointed. "I have to be there though, you know, being the head of church legal council and everything."

"I'm sorry Darian, I just can't face it all."

"You don't have to face it alone, I'll be right there with you," he assured her.

"I can't. I came to this church because I saw how big it was. I thought that I could just fall in with the crowd, and no one would ever even acknowledge me. I didn't plan for all of this."

"But it was God's plan all along. Stand up to adversity, I know you've got it in you. You're strong, you've proven that."

"Darian I'm not going okay! If I wanted all of this drama I would have stayed where I came from, I'm sick of being strong, I just don't want to go alright!"

"Nikki if you ran away from home because of what people said, and you're going to run away from this because of what people might say, you're going to be running for the rest of your life."

"Maybe that's my intention," she stated curtly.

"But you have a responsibility—"

"Oh don't get me started on responsibility Darian Wright. I am sick and tired of people telling me what my responsibility is. My responsibility was to act like a grown woman when I was only seven years old, and raise my baby sister, to shelter her. She is only a year younger than me but because I was born a year too soon, it was my responsibility to protect her from drug addicts, grown men, and gangs. I had no one to protect me, no one to make me feel safe because I was born a year too soon. You don't know how many nights I had to lie awake, and wish I'd never been born at all. So I'm sorry, but I've had enough responsibility for one lifetime, so if you want to lay a guilt trip on me, it's not going to work!"

"I'm not trying to lay a guilt trip on you, I'm just saying my father specifically asked for you to be there. All I'm asking is for you to trust someone other than yourself for once in your life."

"Read my lips Darian Wright. I am not going," she crossed her arms.

"Fine," he stood and reached out for her hand. "Come on I'll take you home."

The silent treatment Darian gave Nicolette on the drive home was a deafening screech in her ears. It was so loud that it forced her to get into her car and drive over to the church. The board meeting had already began when she arrived, and she was shaking like the ground beneath her was about to open up and swallow her.

"You've got some nerve showing up here!" A woman hissed at Nicolette just as she was about to enter the sanctuary.

Nicolette tried to ignore her and walk away, but the woman grabbed her arm, "are you crazy let go of me."

"You think just because you got knocked up he's yours but you're wrong!"

"Natalie put your claws away and mind your business. I never did like you," Adrian interjected seeming to appear out of nowhere.

Natalie quickly retreated into the safety of the room where the meeting was being held.

"You know you're either really brave or really stupid," Adrian shook his head. "Do you realize how many women hate you right now?"

"What are you doing out here?" Nicolette demanded.

"Darian thought you might decide to show up, so I was put on guard duty."

"What's going on in there?" she nodded towards the door.

"Let's go see," Adrian opened the door allowing Nicolette to enter then he followed. They slid into the back row virtually unnoticed.

"The church bylaws clearly state that no staff member in this church shall do anything that may jeopardize the reputation of the church. The simple fact is that you hired Nicolette Cotter knowing that she was an unwed mother. What kind of message does that send to the teenage girls in this church?" Deacon Patterson demanded to know. Darian had always said the man was gunning for his father's position, and the determined look in his eyes told everyone he had a plan.

Pastor Wright shook his head, "the message that all have sinned and fallen short of the glory of God. The message that all can be forgiven, no matter what they have done. How many here are qualified to be a member of a church that has no sinners? The Bible says that only one man lived without sin and His name was Jesus!"

"Amen Pastor Wright!" A woman called from the crowd.

"We understand this, however we feel that you may have been able to find a more qualified candidate had you taken time to search our congregation," Deacon Patterson shot him a sinister smile.

"And what qualifications does she have?" Pastor Wright wanted to know.

"I um…" the deacon's smile faded.

"She's efficient, she's organized, and she's qualified."

"If the members of this church pay the secretary's salary don't you think they should have a say in who she is?"

"Excuse me," Darian interjected. "Is Nicolette Cotter the issue at hand today or is Pastor Darius Wright?"

"Pastor Wright naturally."

"Then let's get to the issue at hand and stop playing ring-around-the-rosie shall we?"

Deacon Patterson shook his head in dismay, "you really disappoint me son."

"Oh really?"

"Yes, I have to say I was certainly heartbroken to hear about your indiscretions."

"As I was yours, it's not every day that church legal council has a deacon who owes five years in back child support, and is on his way to jail, but that's beside the point. I mean we are here to talk about the removal of Pastor Darius Wright as church pastor aren't we?"

"Yes sir absolutely," Deacon Patterson gave a nervous nod.

"On what grounds?"

"Jeopardizing the reputation of the church."

"I see," Darian nodded and it clearly made the deacon uncomfortable.

"And who are we nominating for the appointment as new church pastor?"

"Well I didn't encourage it, but some people were suggesting that I'd be a good candidate for the position."

"So the brilliant plan you propose here today Deacon Patterson is that we remove the man who had a vision, and built a church, on a miniscule speculation, without a bit of proof, and then appoint you?"

"Darian we all know this is a bit difficult for you being that your father is the pastor, but we have to think about the health of our church. Your indiscretion shows his inability to raise a child correctly, and if he can't even handle his family affairs then surely he can't handle his responsibilities as the pastor of a church this size."

"But you can correct?"

"Absolutely!"

"Just like you handled your ex-wife by refusing to pay child support for five years, but never mind that, Pastor Darius Wright is the issue at hand."

"Absolutely," Deacon Patterson clearly didn't know what to make of Darian's comments. "The deacons are split, but if the vote does not go in Pastor Wright's favor then I am ready and willing to take over where he left off."

Darian stared at Deacon Patterson long and hard without a word.

"Uh oh there's the look," Adrian whispered.

"What look?" Nicolette wanted to know.

"You'll see," he shook his head in dismay.

"You feel that the reputation of the church is at stake, so let's look at the facts."

"Let's," Deacon Patterson glanced at his watch as though he had somewhere to be.

"How many deacons are voting today?"

"Only nine," Deacon Patterson stated.

"Is that so?" Darian shook his head in an intimidating manner.

"That's what I have on my list."

"Why only nine?"

"Because they were the only ones who signed up by the deadline of noon today to be eligible to vote.

"That's funny I would expect more than nine deacons to have a part in a vote so crucial to the future of this church."

"So would I," Deacon Patterson agreed whole heartedly. "I guess people don't like to get involved when they're unsure of what the outcome will be."

"May I have a look at that list?"

"By all means," he handed Darian the list without hesitation.

"Just as I suspected," Darian chuckled. "Four of these men are sure to vote for Pastor Wright, and the other four against him."

"Maybe so, only time will tell."

"You do realize that you're in a church don't you sir?"

"Are you suggesting that I set this all up?"

"No, not at all. Because if you'd set this up Pastor Wright would lose, but just for my curiosity's sake, let's go ahead and vote. All of those in favor of Pastor Wright being removed as RMBC's pastor raise your hand," five hands including Deacon Patterson went up. And all those against?" The remaining four hands were raised.

"Then it's settled," Deacon Patterson smiled.

"Congratulations Pastor Wright," Darian grinned at his father. You just won by a four-to-one margin. Would you like for me to explain to you why only your vote counted today Deacon Patterson?"

"What?"

"The church bylaws say that for any deacon's vote to count they have to have attended at least seventy percent of the most recent deacon's board meetings. That disqualifies Deacon Warner, Deacon Morrison, and Deacon Brown. As for Deacon Mitchell, he is currently not only a Deacon at Mt. Olive Baptist Church, but he is also engaged to the pastor's daughter. Congratulations on your engagement, however your affiliation at that church, thus exhibiting your commitment to another church, disqualifies your vote."

"But..." Deacon Patterson shook his head in disbelief.

"Now that that's been taken care of. On to the next issue at hand. The church bylaws clearly state that over one-half of the deacon board or three-fourths of the congregation at any gathering have the right to vote a deacon out of their position. I propose the removal of Deacon Patterson as a deacon at this church on the grounds of staging a vote that did not give the deacons adequate time to sign up to be a part of it, thus jeopardizing the health of the church.

"I second that," Pastor Wright raised his hand and the church erupted into a screaming and applauding frenzy.

"That won't be necessary, effective immediately I resign," Deacon Patterson barked.

"Meeting adjourned," Deacon Turtle cheered with glee.

"Still the man!" Adrian gave a clap, and then took Nicolette's hand and pulled her to her feet. They weaved through the crowd and made their way up front.

"There's my girl," Darian's eyes lit up when he saw Nicolette.

"Congratulations gentlemen," Deacon Turtle shook hands with Pastor Wright and nodded towards Darian. "But Darian, aren't you worried about your reputation now that this has come out?"

"False accusers don't intimidate me."

"Are you saying the baby's not…" Deacon Turtle lowered his voice.

"Let's just agree that God always has a plan," Pastor Wright cut in.

"Amen!" Deacon Turtle and Evelyn rang in unison.

Chapter Six

"You look exhausted," Darian stroked Nicolette's cheek as he pulled up in front of the church. They had just left her five month checkup, and Darian proudly held the sonogram picture of the baby she carried.

"Darian I'm fine," Nicolette unbuckled her seatbelt and Darian hopped out of the car and rushed over to help her out of the car.

"I can do it," she grumbled.

"But you don't have to," he helped her up with a grin. Now that they were openly dating and she was starting to show, Darian had been like a bodyguard.

Nicolette had received enough envious daggers from jealous women to take out half the congregation. She slammed her door shut and nudged Darian, "no one's even here. Back up!"

"Can I show them the picture?" He took her hand and they headed for the church.

"Yeah, it just looks like an alien to me," she shrugged.

"This baby is adorable," he pulled her along and they headed into the church and straight to Pastor Wright's office. "What's up people?"

"Hey how'd it go?" Pastor Wright looked up from his computer.

"Look at this, tell me this is not the most beautiful baby you've ever seen?"

The pastor and first lady began to coo over the ultrasound image.

"Come on man, that thing looks like an alien," Adrian finally spoke out.

"Amen," Nicolette shook her head in agreement.

"So do you Adrian, but you don't hear us complaining," Darian laughed.

"So what is it?" Evelyn asked.

"She told the doctor she didn't want to know," Darian whined.

"What made you decide that?" Pastor Wright asked with his eyes fixed on Nicolette.

"I don't know," she shrugged.

"I already know what it is," Adrian called.

"What?" Darian looked at the photo with his brother.

"A gremlin, look at that big old head. I know that's going to hurt," he grinned. "That baby's going to rip you—"

"Shut up Adrian!" the shouts of everyone in the room caused the baby to jump.

"Wow," she touched the spot on her stomach.

Darian immediately walked over to her and began to rub her belly, "come on now I saw that one."

"Still won't kick for you?" Adrian gave him a sinister smile.

"Adrian don't you have someone else's day to make miserable?"

"Boys," Pastor Wright scolded them.

"What? I can't help it if Nicolette's baby is smart enough to know Darian is an idiot. That baby is already intelligent enough to know that it's better to not have a father, than it is to have to deal with Darian," Adrian shook his head.

"Go straighten up your brother's office," Evelyn demanded.

"Nikki already did," Adrian smiled adoringly at his mother.

"Go clean it again," she spoke between gritted teeth.

"Yes, ma'am," he slid out of the office.

"Shut the door," Evelyn instructed Darian. "Are you still coming to the house tonight?"

"Yes ma'am. I need to go and get a haircut this afternoon though."

"Darian you said..." Nicolette stopped herself.

"What?"

"Never mind," she huffed. He had been promising her for weeks that they would do something special the day she had her ultrasound appointment.

"Oh," realization filled Darian's eyes. "Nikki don't be mad at me, we'll have a good time with my parents tonight."

"If you had other plans Darian it's alright," Pastor Wright offered.

"No," he shook his head. "You fit us into your busy schedule, we'll be there."

"Alright then," he grinned at his son.

"Nikki I'm going to the barbershop, I'll be back to pick you up later," he dismissed her with his eyes.

"Maybe I can get Adrian to take me home," she walked out of the room.

"Nikki I'm sorry," Darian followed her down the hall.

"If you're having second thoughts about this relationship then you have the luxury of backing out of this."

"What are you talking about? You know I'm excited about this baby," he touched her shoulder.

"Don't touch me!" She snatched away.

"Let's go to my office and talk," Darian pleaded with her.

"No!" She snapped as he pushed her into the office and shut the door.

"Nikki stop," he got in her face. "Stressing out is not good for you or the baby."

"I know he ain't hit that yet, but I hope you at least felt on this dude because I think he got the same thing between his legs as you," Adrian laughed.

"Adrian don't start with me," Darian boomed. "Baby listen to me, I told my parents that today was going to be special for you, and they just wanted to be a part of it. My mom went shopping yesterday, maybe she got something for the baby."

"Darian it's not about your parents. You decided that we would have dinner with your parents tonight, and didn't say a word to me," she dared him to deny it.

"You're right, I couldn't say no. I'm sorry," he sighed.

"Like I said, no balls. You better make sure he's still a man down there before things get serious between the two of you. Imagine your surprise on your wedding night when you realize that you're a lesbian," Adrian laughed again.

"Would you get out?" Darian pointed to the door.

"Alright, you don't have to tell me twice. I have a lunch date anyway."

"Adrian can you take me home later?" Nicolette asked as he opened the door.

"Of course I can," Adrian rubbed his hands together with a mischievous grin.

"Actually he'll have to take you to my apartment, I got a dress picked out for you over there."

"Uh-oh," Adrian shook his head.

"So not only did you not tell me we were going to spend the night with your parents, you've known for long enough to pick out what I'm going to wear."

"Some of your dresses are a little short. I just want you to look nice, besides you're not as small as you used to be. You need to wear something you'll be comfortable in."

"It's freezing out there, who told you I was going to wear a dress anyway?"

"You're not in south Florida anymore, you'll get used to it."

"How long have you known about this Darian?"

"Not long, and I said I was sorry, so I don't know what the big deal is."

"The big deal is that I don't like for people to change my plans, and not include me, when I'm expected to be involved. If I didn't like your parents I wouldn't go."

Darian laughed and it annoyed her, "I love you."

"I really don't want to hear that right now," she looked over at Adrian who was smiling at her.

"Shut the door," he pointed at his brother. "I love you. If I'd known you'd get this upset, I would have told you. When I told my mom how important this ultrasound was to us, she took it and ran with it. I just didn't know how to tell her I wanted this night to be just the two of us, but I promise you I'll make this up to you." He wrapped his arms around her, and pulled her in close, "maybe we can still go somewhere tonight after we leave my parent's house."

"I know how your mother is, I understand. I just wish you would have told me."

"I didn't know how," he kissed her on the cheek. "I didn't want you to feel like I was choosing my parents over you."

In his arms it was easy for Nicolette to forget why she was upset in the first place, "I love you."

"I know," he squeezed her and the baby began to shift. "Did it just move?"

"Yes," she nodded.

"I felt it," he placed his hand on the spot just in time to feel the kick. "He kicked me."

"Of course he kicked you, your brother's been saying all along that he doesn't like you," Nicolette teased.

"He knows his daddy's voice," Darian rubbed her stomach and the baby kicked again.

"Maybe he does," Nicolette wasn't too comfortable with Darian referring to himself as daddy, but she didn't push the issue.

"So are we assuming it's a boy now?"

"We could call the baby it for the next few months," Nicolette smiled.

"We can't call the baby *it*, I want to know what it is, I don't think I can wait."

"You don't have a choice," she spoke with finality. "Meanwhile baby It Cotter will have to do."

"You mean It Wright," Darian laughed and Nicolette joined in. "Even with my parents tonight is still going to be special."

"Every night with you is special," she straightened his tie.

He smiled, "I need to go, but I'll see you in a little bit alright?"

"Yeah," she nodded as he headed out the door.

"So," Adrian broke the silence about half-way through the ten minute drive from the church to Darian's apartment. "Are you excited about this baby thing yet?"

"It's becoming a reality that's for sure," Nicolette responded looking out the window.

"My baby brother is excited enough for the both of you and then some," he shook his head at the thought.

"Your brother's a good guy," she smiled.

"I know he is," Nicolette could tell Adrian wanted to say more.

"But what?"

"Do you love him?"

"Yes," she said with confidence.

"I love my little brother, but he's been taken advantage of more times than I can count. Don't get me wrong, you seem like a nice girl, but I don't want him heartbroken over all this."

She looked at Adrian in a new light, "so that's why you're so obnoxious when I come around? You think I'm using your brother because I'm pregnant?"

"Well, if the maternity pants fit..." He was as calm as a river, yet as serious as a heart attack.

"That thought never even crossed my mind. I actually tried to run from your brother at first," she admitted. "I liked him, but I didn't know what his intentions were in the beginning. Men in the church have a tendency of thinking that pregnant women and women with children are easy."

"What I'm trying to say is I'm sorry for never even giving you a chance. Today when you two were in the office I could see that you were just as into him as he was into you."

"Hearing that from you really means a lot to me," tears filled her eyes.

"Oh don't start that crying," he shook his head. "Pregnant women need to learn to control their emotions."

Nicolette laughed, "if it makes you feel any better I'm not trying to steal your little brother, I just want to be in his life."

"Man he loves you more than he loves my mom and that's saying a lot. He even loves you more than he loves Midnight."

"The one thing more obnoxious than you are is Midnight."

"You can't stand him either?" Adrian smiled at the thought.

"Just like this world has mentally challenged humans, it has mentally challenged dogs, and that dog's got some deep rooted issues."

"Maybe when you have your baby he'll quit treating that dog like a person, I can't stand it when he does that. That dog takes a bath everyday and Darian brushes the dog's teeth twice a day!"

"Are you serious?"

"Did Darian tell you the stupid mutt slept in a crib until he was a year old?"

"No," she shook her head.

"What I don't get is why in the world a dog would want to walk around..."

"With a blankie!" They finished the sentence together and fell into laughter.

"When I left home after I found out I was pregnant I left my grandmother and little sister behind. Jillian is only a year younger than me, but as naïve as a ten year old. I've always been protective over her, and now that I'm gone I have a bad feeling that a lot of guys are going to take advantage of her. I would hope that they wouldn't, but it's the world we live in. I don't want anyone doing it to my sister, and I wouldn't dare do it to another person. I love Darian."

"Why don't you call them?"

"I promised myself that I would never look back, it's hard, but I think it's the best decision I can make for myself."

"Take it from me, sometimes never doesn't last forever. I never thought I'd be twenty-two and depending on my parents because I can't keep a job. Darian used to say he'd never go to church once he turned eighteen, and next to my dad he's the most Godly man I know."

"I said I'd never have a child without a husband."

"Well it is still a possibility that you never will," Adrian smiled. "I think the only reason my brother hasn't asked you to marry him is because he thinks you'll say no. But I know it's only a matter of time before he does. Come on I'll help you get up these stairs," Nicolette hadn't realized they were at the apartment until Adrian jumped out of his Toyota Tacoma and rushed around to help her.

"Thank you," Nicolette responded as Adrian took her hand and they walked to the apartment.

Adrian pulled out a key and opened the front door and Midnight came charging towards them barking and jumping, "go somewhere mutt!"

She entered the apartment followed by Adrian, "Darian!"

"Hey," Darian came from the back bedroom. "Midnight go back in your room," the dog took off towards the extra bedroom and Nicolette and Adrian exchanged smiles. "What?"

"Nothing man," Adrian dismissed him.

"Did he behave himself?" Darian gestured towards Adrian.

"We had a nice little conversation about you," Nicolette informed him.

"Whatever he said about me is a lie," Darian glared at his brother.

"Okay I admit it. I lied. Nicolette, Darian doesn't love you and he isn't excited about the baby."

"Then I guess you better take me home," Nicolette smiled at Adrian.

"Wait a minute, he said that I love you?" Darian asked.

"I calls em like I sees em," Adrian shook his head.

"Nikki you know I love you," he kissed her on the cheek.

"Whipped," Adrian imitated a whip being swung in his brother's direction.

"You're like a sister to me," he embraced her.

"Darian let me holler at you for a minute play boy," Adrian scratched his head in confusion.

"She's like family, she won't tell. You can say what you need to say right here," Darian assured him still holding Nicolette.

"No, I can't," he looked at Nicolette. "You alright Ma?"

"Fine," Darian's words had thrown her for a loop. She wasn't sure if he'd said it because Adrian was there, or because he'd met someone else. That morning he certainly hadn't been acting like he thought of Nicolette like a sister.

"Hey there's a couple of dresses on my bed. Go ahead and change while I talk to my brother," he released her and gave her a quick peck on the cheek.

From the moment Nicolette met up with Darian at the apartment his entire attitude had changed. Even his parents noticed the difference that night at dinner. There was no doubt in her mind that somewhere between the time he'd left the church that morning and the time they'd arrived at his apartment he'd met another woman. She'd gone from girlfriend to girl friend in a matter of hours and there was a huge difference in the way he treated her. He'd gone from openly affectionate to cordial.

"Son is there a problem?" Pastor Wright asked as he pushed the plate which had been cleaned of the sweet potato pie on it in less than a minute flat.

"No," Darian eyed him nervously. "Nikki's had a long day, I think I need to get her home."

"Darian," Evelyn called his name firmly and he sat up straight.

"Not now mom, I can't," he shook his head.

"Can't what?" Nicolette asked feeling like she was the only one in the dark.

"Call me in the morning dad," Darian stood.

"Nikki's not done with her pie," Evelyn pointed to her plate.

"She doesn't need it do you?" Darian put his hand on her shoulder.

"Son I need to speak with you about something before you go," Pastor Wright stood and Darian followed him out of the room.

"Nikki is everything alright between the two of you?" Evelyn asked once they were gone.

"I think the sonogram put things in perspective for your son."

"What do you mean by that?"

"He said he loves me like a sister," Nicolette told her with tear-filled eyes. "I don't know why I thought he would want to be anything more to me."

"Nikki the last thing that man wants to be is your brother," Evelyn spoke with confidence.

"Somewhere between the time he left the church this morning, and the time Adrian dropped me off at his apartment something happened. He's been acting strange."

"Ready to go?" Darian asked Nicolette.

She stood without a word.

"Nikki take the day off tomorrow, I have some things I need to take care of, and I don't really have anything left for you to do until next week."

"Thank you Mrs. Wright," she nodded. "Goodnight."

"Goodnight," Darian said as he led Nicolette to the door and they headed outside. "Are you okay?"

"Fine," Nicolette sighed as she got into Darian's car.

The only conversation during the ride to Nicolette's apartment came from the radio. She kept her eyes out the passenger side window and shed tears in silence as they drove. She wondered if this was payback for her getting upset about him not telling her that she was expected to spend the evening with his parents.

"I guess I'll see you on Sunday," Darian sighed as he sat and waited for her to get out of his car. He didn't even bother to turn off the ignition, and didn't make any attempt to get out of his car. He wasn't even going to walk her to her door.

"What did I do?" Her voice shook as she asked and her eyes still looked out the window towards the night.

"You tell me," he huffed.

"Darian I don't know what you mean," she finally mustered up enough courage to face him. She had nothing to hide.

"Did you have a good time with Adrian today?" Even in the darkness Nicolette could see his smug expression.

"You're jealous," she couldn't believe he was being so childish because she was getting along with his brother.

"I just don't have time for games," he shrugged. "If you want him just say so."

"Goodnight Darian," she hopped out of the car and headed for her front door.

"Nikki wait!" He touched her shoulder as she put her key in the door.

"Oh now you want to talk?" She turned to him with fire in her eyes.

"Yes," he slid the keys from her hands and opened the door. They entered the apartment and Darian locked the door as though he were at home.

"Talk," she folded her arms and awaited an explanation.

"Let's sit," he gestured for her to go to the sofa and she went and had a seat. He followed suit taking the place beside her, "Nikki there are some things about my family that you don't understand."

"Like what?"

"About Adrian," he sighed.

"What about him?"

"I know he's better looking than me."

"By whose standards?" Nicolette asked. From the first day she met them, as far as she was concerned Darian was definitely the better looking brother. Adrian favored their father, which wasn't a bad thing. But Darian had more of his mother's looks, and that was a clear-cut compliment.

"I've been involved with females in the past who have used me to get to Adrian, and I'm not saying that it was your intention, but I just didn't like what I saw when the two of you came to my apartment this afternoon."

"So instead of talking to me you decided to be an asshole for the rest of the day," Nicolette glared at him.

"Please don't speak that way you're a lady," he looked taken aback.

"Well when no other words seem appropriate Darian I'm sorry. You made me feel like crap today, and I don't think I did anything to deserve that."

"It's not you that I don't trust," he took her hand. "It's just that what Adrian wants Adrian gets."

"And what do you think he wants?"

"I know he wants you. I couldn't get him to admit it when you left the room, but I've seen the look he gave you too many times before."

"Darian I'm five months pregnant, nobody wants me…really."

"I do," he protested.

"You made that pretty clear. You love me like a sister right?"

"I just said that because I didn't want you to feel like you were obligated to be with me if you don't want to be."

"You hurt me! This morning you treated me like I was important to you."

"You are."

"Then how come you couldn't just talk to me? If you want to be with someone and something is bothering you, then don't you think you should let them know?"

"You're right," he admitted. "But you don't understand what it's like to be Adrian Wright's brother. Everything I can do he can do better because he taught me everything I know."

"Darian your brother loves you. He drilled me for information on what my intentions were with you because he's afraid that I'm trying to take advantage of you because I might just think that because I'm pregnant I need a man."

"I'm sorry," he caressed her hand. "I love you."

"Then love me enough to tell me when something is wrong."

"I can't believe I messed things up like this," he exhaled and released her hand.

"What do you mean?"

"Come on Nikki, you're a smart girl. I know you probably figured out what I was going to do that was going to make tonight special."

"I thought about it," she smiled.

"I want you to be my wife, but what do you want? What can I do for you that will make you happy?" Darian wrapped his arms around her and pulled her as close to him as he could.

"Spend the night with me," she'd wanted to ask him for a while, but didn't know how.

"I have class tomorrow and I have to get up early."

"I don't care, I want you to stay," she whined.

"Is the baby moving," he was trying to change the subject.

"No, but if you stay I'm sure you'll feel it. The baby moves the most during the night."

"You know I can't spend the night with you, my mom would beat me senseless if she found out."

"I'm not worried about your mother. I want you here with me," she put her hand on top of his.

"And if we do this right we will have every night for the rest of our lives together. I want our relationship to be blessed."

Nicolette rolled her eyes. It was not the response she wanted to hear, "it's not like I'm asking you to do anything. I just want you here. I want to feel your arms around me while I sleep and wake up next to you like the last time."

"Baby we have plenty of time to do that. I don't think you understand just how hard it is for me to be alone with you. It's like asking for something to happen between us. Thank God we work in a church or I'd really be in trouble."

Nicolette removed his hand from her stomach and turned her back to him, "whatever you say."

"Don't get mad," he whimpered.

"I'm not unzip me," he unzipped her dress. "I'm going to take a shower. You can come in if you want to."

Darian looked up, "don't say things like that!"

"Whatever," she kept walking and headed into the bathroom.

"Hey," Darian knocked on the door as she turned on the shower.

"What?"

"I'm leaving, I'll call you."

"Alright just lock the door," she was disappointed, but she understood. Darian was a faithful man of God, and he was not willing to tempt himself.

"I will," she heard him call as she stepped into the shower.

Chapter Seven

Nicolette was sound asleep when the phone shrilled, "hello?"

"I'm sorry, I didn't think you'd be asleep."

"It's alright," she sat up and saw that the rising sunlight was sneaking through her window. "I was hoping you'd call."

"So how was your shower last night?"

"It could have been better if someone would have stuck around," she sighed.

"Now that's just wrong. You know you shouldn't say things like that."

"You know you really shouldn't ask a question like that. What type of question is how was your shower?"

"I was just making conversation," she could hear the smile in his voice. "I miss you already."

"Awww, isn't that sweet?"

"You're not upset with me for not staying are you?"

"No, I understand completely."

"Good," he sounded relieved. "I wanted to talk to you about a few things. Can I come over?"

"Why?"

"Just to talk. I can be there in two minutes."

"Okay," she agreed as she jumped out of bed. "Even though I look a mess."

"Don't try to fix yourself up, I want to see how you look when you wake up in the morning."

"Okay," she said as she began to try to finger comb her hair.

"I'm here come open your door for me," she heard his car door shut.

"You said I had two minutes," she grumbled.

"Come on girl, it's cold out here this morning."

"I'm coming," she rushed to the door and when she opened it he greeted her with a dozen roses in hand. "Darian they're beautiful."

"I'm glad you like them," he beamed as he handed them to her and they headed to the kitchen.

"So what did you want to talk about that couldn't wait until a decent hour?" She asked as she filled a vase with water and arranged the roses in it.

"Come on," he took her hand and led her to her bedroom. "I want you to relax."

"Darian what are you up to?" Nikki was on edge.

"Lie down and relax, you said you wanted me to hold you."

"And you were completely against it, what made you change your mind?"

"Compromise. I couldn't spend the night with you, but I can spend the morning with you."

"Don't you have class?"

"Missing one day won't kill me."

"Missing one day might not kill you, but your mother will. I don't want to be the reason you miss class," she shook her head.

"Then I'll just stay for a little while," he lifted her comforter and pointed to the empty bed while he kicked off his shoes.

"Is there some unwritten law that says it's not alright to get in bed with your girlfriend in the night, but it is in the morning?" She asked as she climbed into bed.

"No, but after I left here last night I went back to my parent's house. After the talk I had with my dad I think I have a little more self-control than I had," he got in bed beside her.

"Darian!" She sat up. "Please tell me you didn't tell him that I asked you to spend the night with me?"

"Nikki he's my pastor and my father. I tell him almost everything," he pulled her back to the pillow and wrapped his arms around her.

"Well this better not be an almost," she grumbled.

"I love you."

"I love you too."

"I want you to feel like you can talk to me about anything."

"I do."

"So I can ask you about anything, and you won't get upset with me like you did the first time I asked?"

"Yes," she said without much confidence.

"I want to know about the baby's father," he exhaled.

"What about him?" Nicolette tried to pull away, but Darian wouldn't allow it.

"How long were the two of you together?"

"A little over a year."

"Does he know about the baby?"

"Yes, I told you he gave me the money to have an abortion."

"I know, and I'm sorry to do this to you. Nikki do you still love him?"

"No, I never really did. I loved the attention he attracted. We went to high school together and he graduated a year ahead of me. He was our local college football star, the guy who every girl wanted, and he chose me."

"Did you get pregnant on purpose?" She felt him loosen his grip a little after the question was asked.

"What do you think I'm going to hit you?"

"I never really know what to expect with you."

"The obvious answer to that question for everybody back home is yes. But no I didn't get pregnant on purpose. He kept pressuring me to have sex with him and every time all I could think about was all of the girls out there who would sleep with him if I wouldn't. There's no doubt in my mind that I wasn't the only one he was involved with. I used to sneak out of my grandmother's house to go and see him and he'd have other females there, and say that they were there for his friends. I finally decided one day that enough was enough and that I would give him what he wanted even if it wasn't what I wanted. A month later I was at the store with my baby sister buying a pregnancy test."

"You got pregnant on your first time?"

She'd told her sister that lie so many times it felt like the truth, "yep."

"That's rough," he sighed. "I damn near killed the first girl I was with when she rejected me."

"Uh oh, Darian Wright said a bad word," Nikki giggled.

"Girl please," he hushed her. "I wasn't always the man I am today, and God's still got work to do on me. Even after all these years just the thought of that girl makes me want to strangle somebody."

"Well I'm with child, so FYI if you strangle me you'll be killing two," Nicolette informed him.

"I would never hurt you."

"It hurt to know that he chose football over me and his child, but that's life," she shrugged.

"Man after my first I followed in the footsteps of my big brother. We ran through so many girls we couldn't even remember their names."

"What made you stop?"

"This girl named Crystal. She seemed so sweet and shy I knew she was meant for me. Adrian told me she was sly and sneaky, but I didn't listen. I stopped running around with any and everyone for six months behind that girl. She decided to give me her virginity for my eighteenth birthday. After that she started avoiding me and a couple of days later I knew why. That hoe gave me gonorrhea."

"Are you serious?"

"Apparently it's a disease that some people don't have symptoms with and she was one. While I on the other hand wasn't so lucky."

Nicolette began to giggle, "you poor baby."

"I'm glad you see the humor in me being on fire. I just think about it and I'm afraid to pee."

Nicolette laughed even louder, "I'm sorry."

"No you're not! I can't believe you're over here cracking up over this, but that's alright. They told me not to have sex for seven days, and it's been two years."

Nicolette continued to snicker, "did you use a condom?"

"No, did you?" He sounded irritated.

Her laughter stopped immediately, "no."

"And you knew this dude had other sexual partners?"

"I know, the stupid things we do," she shrugged. "They tested me for like ten STDs that day they took all that blood from me."

"I remember, you came back to work about to pass out. Speaking of which I finally talked to my dad about putting you and the baby on my insurance, even though I've already done it. He said he didn't know you were paying out of pocket after I sat there and told him! I can't stand it when I talk to people and they don't listen to me!"

"What did you say?" Nicolette asked.

"Funny," he huffed.

Nicolette turned to face him, "feel."

Darian began to rub her tummy and the baby responded with a few jabs, "man he's going to be a fighter."

"Or she," Nicolette reminded him.

"No, you're a little too rough around the edges, I had a talk with God," he continued to rub her bulging belly. "We think it's best if you have all boys."

"So they can grow up to be like you and Adrian?"

"Hey that may not be a bad thing. I'm a good guy," he touted his own horn.

"So do I know your deepest darkest secret now?"

"No, I didn't tell you the worst part about that," he began to tap her stomach.

"How can being burned have a worst part?"

"Adrian told my mom."

"Oh God," the baby began to kick.

"See even the baby knows that's bad news," he laughed.

"What did she do?"

"She whooped my behind, with a belt."

"No she didn't."

"Nikki I was still living at home and I was in my bed asleep. Next thing I knew she was tearing me up. It was a nightmare. I was afraid to pee, I was afraid to sit, and I was afraid to be within ten feet of her. That's the reason I moved out on my own. That's why that troublemaking tattle tale is reaping the seeds he's sown, and can't keep a job to save his life. He always used to tell me to do things, then when I'd do them, he'd tell on me."

"Wasn't he doing the same thing as you?"

"He still is. That man's had seven or eight STDs, and he still hasn't learned his lesson. I just pray he doesn't get something that he can't get rid of. Maybe if he's lucky he'll find a good woman like I did."

"Last night you said that you wanted a wife."

"No," he corrected. "I said I wanted you to be my wife."

"Then why haven't you asked me to marry you?"

"I'm afraid you'll say no," he admitted.

"That's what Adrian said yesterday, but I won't. So ask me," she caressed his cheek.

"I can't," he stared into her eyes.

"Why not?"

"Because you just told me to, it has to be unexpected."

"I love you," she smiled.

"I love you too," he leaned in to kiss her and she turned to offer him her cheek.

"Why do you do that?"

"Do what?"

"I've kissed you ninety-seven times and you never let me kiss you on the lips."

"You counted?"

"Yes, but that's not the point, why do you always turn your head?"

"I don't know where your mouth has been Mr. Gonorrhea."

"That's dirty Nikki. I thought you loved me."

"I do, and I hope you love the taste of bleach if you think I'm going to kiss you at a wedding."

"That's not funny."

"It's not supposed to be."

"Can we leave my past in my past?"

"We could have before you told me you were a manwhore, now that ship has sailed. A cap full of bleach."

"Only if you do it first," he smiled.

"I have," she sighed.

"When? It better not be since you've been pregnant," he sat up.

"I'm joking Darian calm down."

"But seriously do people actually drink bleach?"

"I don't know."

"Now that we're being honest with one another and whatnot I have another serious question for you?"

"What?"

"Can you cook?"

"Baby I can burn," she smiled.

"Now is not the time for figures of speech Nikki, for real. Wright men like to eat, and my mom wanted to know if you'd help her with Thanksgiving dinner."

"Of course I will," Nikki cooed.

"Don't embarrass me now, you know they'll talk about you if you do."

"You never know. I might teach your momma a thing or two in the kitchen."

"Now that I'd love to see," he kissed her on the cheek.

Chapter Eight

"Amen," rang through the Wright family dining room as Pastor Wright finished giving a soulful blessing to the Thanksgiving feast Nicolette and Evelyn had prepared.

"Wait a second," Darian stopped Adrian as he was about to dig in. I just wanted to say something else real quick."

"Come on man, a brother is hungry, everybody knows that if you get to preaching we'll never eat," Adrian objected.

"I just wanted to say that I am thankful that this year instead of the four of us, Nikki could join us. I definitely have more to be thankful for this year than most, and this time next year I look forward to having a baby here to be a part of this."

"I don't," Adrian cut in. "Crying and making all that noise at the table while a brother's trying to get his grub on."

"Shut up Adrian!" Evelyn spat.

"Nikki if you can put up with my family, especially my beloved brother for as long as you have then you are a good woman. I don't want to miss out on the opportunity to be with you forever, so I want us to let the world know what we already know. That we were meant for each other."

"Get on your knee boy," Evelyn instructed.

"Let the boy have his moment," Pastor Wright scolded her.

Darian slid off of the chair onto his knee, "will you marry me Nicolette Lillian Cotter?"

"Here come the tears," Adrian called out before Nicolette could answer.

"Shut up Adrian!" Nicolette barked. "This is my moment."

"You taught her well son," Pastor Wright chuckled.

"Yes, I'll marry you," she smiled down at him.

"I guess it would help if I took the ring out of my pocket," he pulled out a case and slid a diamond ring out, then gently glided it onto her finger.

"How you afford that?" Adrian asked as he peered over at the ring.

Nicolette wondered the same thing, but didn't have the nerve to ask, "it's beautiful."

"This girl is priceless big bro!" Darian rose and took his seat.

"Maybe so but the bling in that ring is pricefull," Adrian grinned.

"I love you Nikki," he smiled adoringly at her.

"I love you too Darian," she grinned at him.

"Man that sucked. He got you that big old diamond and he didn't even get a kiss for it. Can we eat now?"

"I can't wait to tell Midnight," he smiled at Nicolette and she reluctantly smiled back.

"You might as well go ahead and tell him you don't like his dog girl," Adrian laughed. "You in good company though, we don't like him either."

"Actually he's growing on me," she admitted. "A little."

"I knew he would, he's a good kid."

"He's not a kid he's a dog for crying out loud!" Adrian hollered.

"Adrian that is enough!" Evelyn yelled at him.

"Sorry," Adrian apologized. "We better eat, Georgia College is playing Southwest Florida University today."

"On Thanksgiving Day? That's a first," Pastor Wright commented.

Everyone began to dig in except for Nicolette. Adrian's last comment was like a tornado spinning off of memory lane headed straight for her.

"Nikki are you alright?" Darian asked when he realized she was not eating.

"I think so," she held her stomach as a ploy.

"That feeling is your baby telling you not to marry this clown," Adrian began to laugh, but was cut off by the look Evelyn gave him.

"Maybe you're just hungry," Evelyn offered. "You have been on your feet a lot this morning."

"Yeah," Nicolette agreed as she slowly began to eat.

"Well it's official," Pastor Wright was eating like a starving wolf and had devoured half of the food on his plate in a matter of seconds. "The girl can cook."

"Amen," Adrian agreed with a full mouth and a nod. "Giving the old lady some competition up in here."

"Nikki you have chills are you sure you feel alright?" Darian touched her arm.

"Darian take her to the guest room and let her lie down," Evelyn told him.

"Come on," he stood and helped her up leading her down the hall to the spare room.

"I think I'll be alright."

"Lie down," he ignored her and she did as she was told. "Now this is just the two of us, is there something you would like to tell me?"

"No," she said as her eyes teared up.

"Are you sure?" He sat beside her on the bed.

"I know I want to marry you," she told him.

"I know you do too, that's not what I'm talking about. Adrian said something and your whole demeanor changed. Are you sure you don't want to talk about it?"

"Yes," she took his hand in hers and kissed it. "I love you."

"Alright, I'll be back to check on you, try to take a nap for me. You look exhausted."

"I will," she grinned.

"Nikki wake up baby," Darian shook her and she opened her eyes.

"Hey," she stretched and realized she had fallen asleep in the guest room.

"There's someone here to see you, can I send him in?"

"Yes," she shrugged unsure of who could possibly want to see her.

Darian disappeared and moments later Jarvis Davis was standing in the doorway.

"What are you doing here?" Nicolette sat up in horror.

"I had a game in town, and thought I'd drop by to check on you. It's mighty funny I gave you two thousand dollars to have an abortion and here you are as pregnant as can be."

"I was going to, I just couldn't."

"I don't want your excuses! You're not getting a dime from me, so you might as well just give that up!"

"I don't want your money Jarvis. I'm engaged," she held out her now ringless finger.

"That man doesn't want you," Jarvis laughed.

"Darian!" She stood and Jarvis blocked her exit.

"I'm right here baby," Darian caressed her cheek and she opened her eyes.

She sat up and looked towards her ring finger and saw that the ring was still there, "I thought you were gone."

"Well this is my parent's house," he smiled. "Are you ready to talk yet?"

"Where is everyone?"

"In the living room watching the game," she knew he was gauging her for a reaction. She didn't know how he'd figured her out, but it was obvious he had.

"How'd you know?"

"When you love someone you just know some things," he smiled. "Do you feel comfortable watching it?"

"I don't care about him!" She snapped.

"Come on," they went to the living room hand in hand and Darian took a seat pulling Nicolette down beside him. "What did I miss?"

"Your school fumbled the ball," Adrian sucked his teeth. "They suck."

"Nikki I'll go and fix you a plate, you still haven't eaten," Evelyn told her.

"Awww man!" Darian howled.

"Damn!" Adrian yelled. "That's it for his season."

"Watch your mouth boy!" Pastor Wright warned.

"What happened?" Evelyn asked looking towards the screen.

"Nikki get up baby," Darian tried to distract her from the screen. "Look at me."

"They have to show that again, check it out," Adrian pointed to the TV.

"Nikki," Darian tapped her shoulder, but she ignored him.

"And that's your play of the day!" Adrian belted out with a clap.

"Look at that his leg is broken," Pastor Wright said pointing to the screen.

"And he has to have a concussion from that hit, his helmet flew at least fifteen yards. That's exactly why they need to pay these college boys, they get all hurt up and have nothing to show for it!" Adrian shook his head as they began to show the replay.

Nicolette jumped up and ran for the bathroom making it to the toilet just before she started to throw up.

"Nikki are you alright?" Darian asked.

"No," she said while catching her breath. She began to cry and Darian caressed her.

"Hey she okay?" Adrian was at the bathroom door. "I didn't know you had such a weak stomach."

"No it's not that. Nikki we have to talk about this," Darian sighed.

"I don't want to," she cried on his shoulder.

"Get up," he helped her to her feet and flushed the toilet. "Wash your face."

"Darian?" Adrian seemed concerned as he watched her wash her tear streaked face.

"She's alright man, don't worry about it," Darian assured his big brother.

"What about you?" Adrian's question clearly caught Darian off guard.

"I'll be alright," he huffed. He took her hand and led her to the guest room. "Dad can you come in here for a minute?"

"I'm fine Darian," she assured him.

"Maybe you are, but I'm not," he told her.

"You need me son?" He asked as he stood in the doorway.

"Come in and shut the door please," Darian kissed Nicolette's hand. "Dad what is said in here is between the three of us. I don't even want mom involved."

"What's going on?" He asked as he shut the door.

"Nikki I love you, I have every intention of marrying you and taking care of you and this baby. My dad is your pastor, just like you feel comfortable with me and can tell me anything, I want you to have the same relationship with him. If he gives you his word he'll keep it, just like I will."

"Nikki would you like to talk to me?" Pastor Wright's seriousness scared her.

"No," she shook her head vigorously.

"Can I tell him?" Darian sat on the bed and she sat beside him.

"Yes," she leaned on his shoulder.

"Nikki told me the baby's father gave her two thousand dollars to have an abortion, and that's why she ended up moving here. He was a star football player who wasn't ready for a family, and today when Adrian mentioned us playing Southwest Florida University, I was probably the only one who really noticed her reaction."

"Darian there are plenty of star football players in Florida. It's a nesting ground for talent."

"But it's him isn't it?"

Nicolette nodded.

"Are you alright?" Pastor Wright asked.

"Yes sir," she nodded again.

"He's hurt pretty bad, do you think you'll want to see him?"

"Dad!" Darian hollered.

"Darian we've talked about this, it's her decision not yours."

"I don't want to see him," Nicolette sighed. "I just tried to block him out of my mind, and this is not helping."

"Have you forgiven him?"

"Yes," she sighed.

"We've been talking about this, and my dad thought that it was best to ask him to terminate his rights if we ever found him."

"Again this is your choice Nicolette, not ours," Pastor Wright gave her a confident smile.

"I don't think he will," a tear rolled down her cheek and Darian wiped it away.

"I still love you and there's no doubt in my mind that I want to spend the rest of my life with you," he kissed her on the hand.

"When young couples come to me with a problem the first thing I ask them to do is pray about it together. I can lead you or I can leave you in here to do this together, but that's the only way to go about it."

"I think we'll be alright alone," Darian looked at his father.

"I know you will," he gave Darian a pat on the back before he left them to be alone.

They held hands and Darian slid down onto his knees, "you ready to do this?"

"As long as I can do it with you," she followed his lead.

Chapter Nine

Darian unlocked his front door and they both entered the apartment. "Midnight I'm home!" he called.

Nicolette rolled her eyes. She was sick of Darian treating a dog like a person.

Midnight came rushing towards Darian and stopped when he saw Nicolette. He looked back and forth between Nicolette and Darian and then turned and went back towards his room.

"Midnight what's wrong?" Darian asked as though he expected the dog to answer.

Midnight nodded in Nicolette's direction then stared at Darian.

"Don't be like that, that's your mom," he smiled as he knelt down and Midnight slowly approached him.

"No I'm not!" Nicolette objected.

Darian cradled him like a baby, "I missed you today."

The dog began to lick Darian's arm in response.

"Disgusting," Nicolette mumbled.

"He's clean, he takes a bath and brushes his teeth everyday," Darian informed her proudly. "Give mommy a kiss."

"I don't kiss dogs," Nicolette backed away. "And please tell me you don't let him lick you in the face."

"Doesn't everyone?"

"Darian I've let you kiss me! That's gross," she tried to shake the thought from her mind.

"I know, I was joking. He licks his own manhood he ain't licking me in the face. Let's go sit," Darian led them to the sofa with Midnight still in tow. "He'll get used to you, he's just a little jealous. He's been acting out since I started dating you. Last night he tore up my running shoes. I guess he's going through the terrible twos."

Nicolette laughed, "if you say so."

"Hold him," Darian extended the dog towards her.

"No thanks."

"Come on, you've never held him. That's why he doesn't want you here. He thinks you don't like him."

"Come here Midnight," Nicolette reluctantly took the dog.

"I have to run to the bathroom, I'll be back," Darian stood and headed for the hallway.

Midnight looked up at her and growled.

"I heard that Midnight!" Darian called and Midnight looked down.

When Nicolette heard the bathroom door shut she looked at Midnight, "get off of me."

Midnight hopped off and growled at her again.

"You don't have to like me, I don't like you either. When I'm done with you you'll be sleeping outside and hooked to a leash and chain."

Midnight dropped his head and walked down the hall whining as though she'd hurt his feelings.

"Where's Midnight?" Darian asked minutes later when he returned.

"I thought he went down the hall looking for you," Nicolette responded innocently.

"Midnight!" Darian sat back beside her. "He has to get used to you since you're going to be around a lot more."

"If he doesn't want to don't force him Darian."

Midnight returned and barked at Darian.

"Don't be like that Midnight, you make me look bad. You know I raised you better than this," Darian opened his arms and the dog climbed onto his lap. "I love you. Give your mom a kiss."

Midnight leaned in Nicolette's direction then snapped towards her and back to Darian.

"Ouch, he bit me," Nicolette rubbed her arm.

"What is wrong with you man?" Darian held the dog up in the air and stared up at him. He stood up with Midnight in his arm, "you eat your dinner and you go to bed!"

Nicolette looked at her bleeding wrist, "Darian does he have all of his shots?"

"Yes," she could hear him pouring food into the dog food bowl.

She stood and walked down the hall to his bathroom. She turned on the water and rinsed her arm.

"Are you bleeding?" Darian looked over her shoulder. "I didn't realize he bit you that hard, I thought he just nipped you,"

Darian took her arm from under the running water. "Let me get the first aid kit."

"I think it stopped bleeding," Nicolette told him when he came back.

"Here," he took her hand and looked at it.

"You must be crazy," she nodded towards the bottle of alcohol in his free hand.

"I need to clean it," he gripped her hand tighter when she resisted.

"I just rinsed it," she argued.

"But you have to disinfect it too."

"No!" She pulled away and stumbled backwards.

"See, you're going to hurt yourself," he put the bottle down. "Go sit down in the living room, I have wet wipes in my bedroom I can get."

When Nicolette returned to the living room Darian was on her heels, "I want to do it."

"No," he flopped down beside her and took her hand gently rubbing the wipe on her wrist.

"It burns!" She snatched her hand away from him shaking it.

"Let me blow," he reached for her arm and she stood.

"I told you no alcohol!"

Darian stood and began to blow on her arm, "I just wanted to make sure it was clean, Midnight has all of his shots, but he's been chewing on everything lately. Sit down and I'll put this pad on it," he pulled her to her seat.

"It's not that bad," she watched as he wrapped it and put adhesive tape on it.

"Listen he's crying," Darian shook his head. "He's not used to me yelling at him."

"Did you lock him in the room?"

"No, I just unplugged his TV, and gave him dog food. When he gets dog food he knows he's in trouble."

"So what does he eat?"

"Whatever I eat," Darian shrugged. "I told you that's my baby."

Midnight began to howl loudly.

"Let him out," Nicolette shrugged.

"No, he has to be punished when he does something wrong. He's never bitten anyone. Not even Adrian and there is no one in this world Midnight hates more than Adrian."

"Well if he's going to be growling and biting he can't be around my baby," Nicolette rubbed her belly.

"He won't I promise. I just need to talk to him."

She shook her head, "you're serious?"

"I know it sounds crazy, but Midnight is very intelligent. Everyone underestimates what my baby knows. He really understands everything I say to him."

"Owwwwwwwww," Midnight howled.

"Darian just let him out."

"No," he shook his head. "He did wrong and he's going to be disciplined for it. Besides there is a reason I wanted you to come over."

"Well Mr. Wright, what is it that you wanted to talk to me about?" Nicolette leaned her head onto his shoulder.

"Us," he sighed and it gave her a bad feeling in the pit of her stomach.

"Okay, so talk."

"You said you went Christmas shopping," he sniffed.

"Yeah, I got your parents tickets to the gospel play coming next month, and your brother a gas card since he's always begging for gas money. I even got a chew toy for Midnight, but his stubborn father still won't tell me what he wants."

"I finally thought of something."

"What?" She closed her eyes and hoped she could afford whatever he wanted.

"You," he brushed his lips against her forehead.

"You've already got me," she opened her eyes and looked up at him.

"No," he shook his head in disagreement. "I mean I want…you."

"Wow," she moved away. She'd tried this man time and time again and now he was saying he wanted her for Christmas. "I thought you wanted to wait."

"I did, but then I thought about it. I know we're going to be together for the rest of our lives, so what's the point in waiting?

Let's just take our relationship that one step further, so that we can move on. I love you and I know you love me."

"I really don't know what you expect me to say," she was completely confused.

He'd just completely shattered her image of him being the most committed man of God she'd ever met unwilling to make any sacrifices that would detract from his faith, "I know you're probably afraid, I know I am, but this is right. This is what God wants. I can feel it."

"Darian I really don't think this is what God wants us to do," she disagreed.

"Yes Nikki it is," he spoke with certainty.

"Have you really thought about this?"

"Yes! I've even discussed it with my parents and my dad is all for it. My mom has her objections, but she wouldn't be Evelyn Wright if she didn't make things difficult."

"Hold up now, wait a minute Darian! You discussed this with your mom and dad?"

"Yes, this afternoon."

"And your father said it's alright?"

"Of course, why wouldn't he. He adores you."

"Oh headache," Nicolette began to massage her forehead. "But Darian he's a pastor."

"I know isn't it great to have his blessing?"

"No," Nicolette exhaled. "How can a pastor say it's okay to…to…"

"Nicolette he's a pastor, but he's also a father. One who knows his son is in love."

"But…"

"What are you afraid of?" He forced her to look into his eyes.

Suddenly she gave him a playful nudge on the shoulder, "I thought you were serious. You were testing me."

"I wouldn't joke about something like this," the humorless look on his face alarmed her. "We don't have to do it on Christmas Day, we can even do it before then if we want to, my dad is willing to cancel whatever he has planned on the day that we choose and this is his busiest time of year."

"Why would he do that?" Nicolette was wondering what kind of freak she'd gotten involved with, and why she hadn't seen this coming.

"He's going to officiate it of course, I wouldn't want to be married by any other person."

Nicolette started to cackle, "I am such an idiot."

"What?" Darian was still in the dark.

"Baby," she composed herself. "When you said you wanted me I thought you meant…"

"Girl get your mind out of the gutter!" Darian shook his head. "Although that is a benefit of getting married."

"You almost gave me a heart attack when you said your father said it was okay," she placed her hand on her chest.

"What did you think my dad was taking the day off so he could watch?"

"I was starting to wonder," she shuddered.

"My mom's going to try to talk us out of it, but I really want to get married in the next couple of weeks. She wants to wait until the baby is born so she can plan a big wedding with a bunch of people she doesn't even like. I just don't want this baby born to an unwed mother. He has a father who loves him and is going to be there for him from day one."

"You are determined to make this a boy aren't you?"

"I think that deep down inside every man who wants kids wants a son. Someone to take after him."

"Isn't Midnight your son?" she teased.

"Yeah, he's my little man trapped in a dog's body."

"Darian let him out that whining is distracting," Nicolette felt sorry for him.

"Oh!" Darian exclaimed. "No wonder he's fussing, his blankie is out here," Darian stood grabbing his blankie and headed back to the bedrooms. "Nikki take him he won't do anything to you," Darian had a panicked expression.

"What's wrong?" She took the half asleep dog from him.

"We have to take him to the emergency vet, he's got diarrhea and there's blood all over his room," Darian snatched up his keys.

Nicolette watched as Darian sat beside her in the waiting room with his eyes closed no doubt deep in prayer. She'd even prayed that Midnight would be alright. As she held the dog she despised in her arms on the way to the vet's office he stared into her eyes and whimpered as though he were begging for help. She felt a connection with him, and she realized how much it would devastate Darian if something happened to him.

"Nikki," Darian jarred her from her thoughts.

"Yeah?"

"If you want I can call someone to come and take you home," he pulled out his cell phone.

"No," she shook her head. "I'm not leaving you like this."

"I've only had him for two years, but he's never been sick. I don't know if I've ever been this terrified in my life. I can't lose him."

"You won't Darian, it's going to be alright," she spoke the words in an attempt to comfort him, but she wasn't so sure.

"I love you Nikki, you're always there for me," he took her hand and kissed it gently. "Have you thought about what I said at the apartment?"

"I want to be with you, but if I say yes to it your mother is going to resent me."

"Don't worry about her. She is in no position to have a say over when I get married. I don't want this baby to be born to an unwed mother, and there's no reason for him to be. I don't know how you feel about it, but I want the baby to have my last name."

"Darian I really don't want you to worry about that right now," Nicolette caressed his hand.

"If not now, then when? My mother is going to be tracking you down like a bloodhound, so I might as well talk to you before she does. If you don't want to get married before Christmas I want it to be your decision not my mother's."

"I just don't want her to despise me for going against her."

"My mom would die a thousand deaths if she knew what I was about to tell you," Darian sighed. "Nikki I don't know the man who fathered me."

"What do you mean? Pastor Wright—"

"Is Adrian's father."

"I thought Adrian was two years older than you," Nicolette thought aloud.

"He is, and my parents were married before he was born."

"But," Nicolette was puzzled.

"She cheated on him," Darian confirmed. "According to Pastor Wright, ironically I saved their marriage."

"You're named after him right?"

"Yeah, my birth certificate even says Darius Wright as my father, but my grandmother told me he wasn't my dad before she passed away five years ago. When I asked Pastor Wright if it was true he told me it was."

"So you never met your father?"

"Nope, my grandmother told me he may have been some attorney named Edward Mitchell, she says I look like him. He was a married man with a family, and most likely knows I exist, but has never attempted to contact me."

"I always thought you just looked more like your mother, and Adrian looks more like your father."

"That's what everyone assumes," he shrugged.

"So that's why you love law?"

"No, I've been interested in law since I was eight years old. I didn't find out about Darius not being my father until I was fifteen. You know by now that my mom is all about appearances, that's probably why she's so protective about who I date. She doesn't want this to get out," he searched her eyes for a judgmental response.

"I can understand why," there was no harsh judgment in her tone.

"Excuse me, Mr. Wright?" A vet tech approached them.

"Yes," Darian stood. "Did they find out what's wrong with him?"

"Yes, it appears that he chewed something plastic. The sharp pieces that he swallowed cut the inside of his stomach and that is what caused the bleeding."

"Will it pass through his system?" Darian wanted to know.

"Most likely yes, but he still needs surgery in order to stitch one of the lacerations in his stomach."

"So he'll need anesthesia?"

"Yes," she nodded. "The sooner we do the surgery the better his chances of survival. We can do the procedure in the morning if you'd like."

"That would be great," he tried to sound upbeat, but Nicolette knew he was worried. "Can I see him now?"

"Yes, follow me," she began to walk away and Darian reached for Nicolette's hand. She took them to a room where Midnight was lying in a cage.

"Is he in a lot of pain?" Darian wanted to know.

"No, he's on enough medication to get him through the night."

"Thank you," he exhaled.

"You're welcome, take all the time you need and we'll see you in the morning," she handed him a file and left the room.

"Midnight," Darian said his name and he lifted his head. He opened the cage and picked up his dog. "I'm here."

"Hey Midnight," Nicolette rubbed the dogs head and it began to lick her.

"I don't think he's going to make it," Darian cradled the dog like a child.

"Darian please don't say that," she begged.

"I should have noticed this," he shook his head. "I knew he was acting strange."

"He'll be fine."

"Whether he is or not, I'll feel better knowing that I have you."

"You have to think positively."

"Anesthesia is way more dangerous with dogs than it is with humans. Even for minor procedures, and there is nothing minor about sewing up a dog's insides."

"I've never heard that before."

"Give me a few minutes then I'll take you home," Darian dismissed Nicolette.

"Take all the time you need," she stroked his cheek with the back of her hand. "See you later Midnight."

Chapter Ten

"Nikki I'm glad you're here early," the smile Evelyn gave her made her want to turn and run away.

"Evelyn stay out of it," Pastor Wright warned.

"Let's go for a little walk," Evelyn ignored her husband with a fake smile plastered on her face.

"Is something wrong?" Nicolette asked nervously.

"No not at all, as a matter of fact I've grown quite fond of you these past few months. I hope I haven't been too much of a nuisance to you."

"No, not at all," Nicolette felt apprehensive about what was to come.

"Nikki I know you love my son, he certainly has committed himself to being devoted to you. Sometimes my son doesn't know what's good for him."

Nicolette's heart skipped a beat, "Mrs. Wright I'm not perfect, but I do love your son and—"

"Let me finish," she was aggressive as usual. "Darian thinks he wants to rush and have a quick wedding, but really the two of you need to wait until after the baby is born. Won't it be nice to take our time and pick out the perfect wedding dress and plan a real wedding instead of a shotgun ceremony?"

"Well…"

"I know Darian can be demanding at times, but you have to hold your ground. That's what I like about you, you aren't a pushover. Tell him you're not ready, tell him you want the baby to be born first. Who knows, if you plan to have the wedding before the baby is born you may be sick that day. That would ruin everything. Darian will understand because he loves you."

"We had a talk last night, he's really adamant about us getting married before the baby is born Evelyn."

"I know," she said with confidence. "And that's why you're the only one who can change his mind."

"Maybe it's selfish of me, but I don't know if I want to change his mind."

"It is very selfish of you. All I want is to be able to plan a big wedding ceremony for my child."

"You do have another child," Nicolette reminded her.

"Who Adrian?" She said as though he meant nothing to her. "What are the chances of him getting married? If by some stroke of miracle he does grow up and decide to quit his foolishness I'll probably be dead by then. Then again with the lifestyle he's living he's bound to die before I do."

"Evelyn with all due respect, this wedding is not just what Darian wants, it's what I want too."

"Then it's settled, let's plan it the right way. Just the two of us. I'll pay for everything."

"What are you two up to?" Darian walked in and Evelyn jumped so hard her skeleton almost popped out of her skin.

"We were talking about you," Nicolette smiled up at Darian.

"Yes," Evelyn gave Nicolette a look that told her to hush, but she ignored it.

"The wedding is kind of short notice," Nicolette stated.

"Didn't we have this discussion last night?" Darian raised a questioning brow.

"Yes but—"

"Nikki you agreed that you'd let me work this all out. I already told you if I'm going to be head of this family you need to let me make the major decisions about the wedding."

Both Nicolette and Evelyn were taken aback. Nicolette figured Darian's father must have filled him in on what his mother was up to, "Darian I don't know if it's appropriate to discuss this in front of your mother."

Evelyn gave her a way to go smile.

"You're right," Darian agreed. "What I say goes, end of discussion."

Evelyn's eyes were so wide her eyeballs were about to pop out of their sockets, "Darian there is no reason for you to speak to her that way."

"Mom if she doesn't learn to submit to authority now then she won't do right when we're married."

"She's a woman, but you still have to respect her. I will be speaking to your father about this," she stormed away.

"What's up with your future monster-in-law?" Darian chuckled once Evelyn was out of sight.

"She wants us to wait until after the baby is born so that she can plan a big wedding."

"But that isn't what we want."

"I want you," she hugged him.

"You've got me baby," he tilted her chin up.

"No kissing in the church," Adrian strolled in all smiles.

"Did mom send you down here to spy on us?" Darian asked.

"No, I just snuck in, I was supposed to be here an hour ago."

"Dad was ticked off with mom when I got here for not minding her business, so it should take some of the heat off of you."

"Darian?" Nicolette suddenly asked.

"Yeah," he smiled at her.

"How is he?"

"He didn't make it," Darian looked down with a frown. "I went over there this morning to see how he was doing and he was gone."

"Darian I'm sorry," Nicolette hugged him and he returned her embrace.

"It's alright, I didn't want him to suffer anyway," he made a failed attempt to sound upbeat.

"Who died?" Adrian suddenly spoke out reminding Nicolette and Darian of his presence.

"Midnight," Darian released Nicolette.

"When? How? Are you alright?" Adrian shot him an array of questions.

"I'm fine," Darian smiled.

"Darian," Nicolette didn't know what to say.

"Let's go back to the office," Darian took Nicolette's hand and Adrian followed them.

The perfect parents were bickering back and forth until Darian walked in and cleared his throat.

"Hey son is something the matter?" Pastor Wright looked back and forth between Nicolette and Darian.

"I can't stay, I have to go and take care of some things," he shook his head. "If you don't have too much for Nikki to do I'd like for her to come with me."

"Has something happened to the baby?" Evelyn asked.

"No," Darian shook his head.

"Darian it's okay to be hurt man," Adrian huffed. "We know you loved him."

"It doesn't matter," Darian was on the verge of tears.

"Who is him?" Evelyn demanded to know.

"Midnight," Adrian responded.

"What happened to Midnight?"

"You don't care," Darian shrugged. "And I don't want to talk about it."

"How'd he die?" Adrian wanted to know.

"Midnight died?" Evelyn asked.

"Excuse me, I need to go and do something in my office," it was obvious he was going to his office to cry, but no one followed him.

"Nikki do you know what happened?" Evelyn turned to her.

"We sat at the Emergency Vet Clinic for two hours last night, and one of the vet techs said it may have been internal bleeding. He seemed fine before we left, so I don't know. Darian tried to call all of you."

"That dog was like his child," Pastor Wright shook his head.

"I know," Nicolette put her hand over the spot where her own child moved.

"Hey Nikki, you do know that I don't mean any harm when I say things to you right?" Adrian asked.

"Yeah," she shrugged.

"Okay, I just wanted to say that for the record. I'm not ready to die."

"What are you trying to say?" Nicolette's tone was razor sharp.

"You couldn't stand that dog."

"So," Evelyn huffed. "Neither could you."

"And the night Darian says he wants to be alone with you, the dog dies."

"Are you suggesting what I think you are?" Nicolette put her hands on her hips defensively.

"I'm saying what no one else in here has the courage to say. You killed Midnight didn't you?"

"What?" Nicolette and Evelyn asked in unison.

"Come on, that dog was two and in perfect health. How else do you explain this?"

"If we weren't in a church I'd—"

"Kill me?" Adrian challenged.

"Your brother is hurting okay, he needed you last night and you were nowhere to be found. Darian knows how I felt about his dog, but I would never do anything to hurt him. Can't you put your asinine comments aside for long enough to realize that your little brother just lost something that means a lot to him? How about comforting him instead of knocking someone else down? You hoe around and you don't see me judging you. Don't judge me, you don't even know me," Nicolette stormed out of the office and headed for Darian's office. She took a deep breath then knocked on the door.

"It's open," Darian called.

"Are you sure you're alright?" Nicolette asked Darian as she opened his door just in time to see him wipe his eyes.

"I will be," he walked over and embraced the woman he loved.

"Son?" Pastor Wright walked into the office.

"Yes sir?"

"Is there anything we can do?"

"No," he shook his head. "Can Nikki come with me?"

"Of course, I'll help your mother if she needs anything."

"Okay, we're leaving then," he let her go and took her hand. They walked past him and headed down the hall.

"Darian?" Pastor Wright called behind them.

"Yes sir?"

"I um," he looked down. "I'm sorry for your loss, I'll be praying for you."

"Thanks," Darian nodded and then turned and they headed out the door.

"Here you go," Nicolette handed Darian a bottle of water and sat down beside him. They had spent the entire day at her apartment, and she was very uncomfortable with the way Darian pretended like nothing out of the ordinary had occurred in his life.

"Thanks," Darian took the bottle and stared at Nicolette for a moment.

"What?"

"You really love me," he smiled.

"Duh," she stroked his cheek.

"You look exhausted, how'd you sleep last night."

"I tossed and turned."

"Were you thinking about Midnight?"

"Yes, and I was worried about you."

"I wish you would have called me," he sighed. "I would have loved to hear your voice."

"I wanted to, but I thought you might want to be alone," she caressed his cheek.

"Come on, I want you to lie down and rest," he stood pulling her to her feet and led her to her bed.

She climbed in bed and looked at Darian, "I love you."

"I know," he began to rub her belly. "You're all I have now."

"No, you have your family."

"They don't care about me," she saw the pain in his eyes. "They just care about the family image."

"Darian they love you just like I do," she pulled him towards her and he climbed under the blanket beside her.

"Then why haven't they called me?"

"Maybe they don't know what to say, Darian I don't know what to say," she suggested in their defense.

"But you're here. You're trying. I loved Midnight. He was my baby, and they all know how much he meant to me, but they don't care."

"Darian calm down," Nicolette felt the baby inside of her pushing harder than ever before.

Darian placed his hand against the movement, "am I stressing him out?"

"No," Nicolette leaned over and kissed Darian on the lips.

"Do you realize what you just did?"

Nicolette automatically assumed she'd done something to offend him, "what?"

"You've never kissed me on the lips," he sighed.

"Darian I love you," she kissed him again.

"I love you too," he leaned over her and kissed her and when she opened her mouth to speak he took it as an open invitation to put his tongue into her mouth.

When he pulled away Nicolette used what little breath she had left to speak, "Darian your hand."

He pushed his hand even harder in between her legs, "you're the only person in this world who really loves me, and I want to make love to you."

"No you don't," she removed his hand and held it between hers. "You don't know what you're saying."

"Nikki I know exactly what I'm saying, just let me show you how much I love you," he placed his hands on her hips and stared into her eyes.

"Darian I really need you to listen to me because I don't have enough self-control to push you away twenty times like you do me," she spoke as his lips roamed down her face and across her neck.

"Then stop fighting it," she gasped when she realized his hand was in her pants.

"Darian quit!" She slapped him with the force of a tennis racquet before she could think twice about it.

He finally sat up rubbing his face with one hand and pulling the other away from her, "why won't you let me do this? You've been trying me for weeks now."

"I know," Nicolette was on the verge of tears. "And I know that you're mad with your parents, and you're mad with your brother, but don't take that out on God. I have never met a twenty year old so dedicated to pleasing God. You have wisdom beyond your years, so use it!"

"Nicolette I have tried so hard these last two years to do everything God asks of me. I go to church, I read and study my Bible, I pay my tithes, I pray, and a lot of times I really feel like I connect to God. I just don't understand why He would allow this to happen to me," Darian began to bawl like a frustrated two year old.

"Darian God makes no mistakes," she pulled him into her arms.

"I just don't understand what I did wrong, what I did to deserve this!" He continued to cry in her arms, "I prayed all night last night and I'm hurt, I'm angry. It feels like God turned His back on me."

"He's testing you Darian, and don't you dare turn your back on Him. My grandmother use to tell me that when things seemed too much to bear, it meant it was time to praise God the most. You were most likely just a praise away from your blessing," it felt good to mention Grandma Dean.

"You're probably right, but it hurts. My heart is broken, I literally feel the pain in my chest Nikki," he sniffed.

"We're a family Darian, let me pray with you," she released him and slid down onto her knees.

"Okay," he whispered as he got down beside her.

She closed her eyes and opened her mouth, and the prayer warrior she'd seen so many times in Grandma Dean came to life in her.

Chapter Eleven

Nicolette sat in church Sunday morning and allowed her mind to wander. The day before had been a very emotional one. Nicolette and Darian had taken Midnight to a pet cemetery where he was buried, and they cleaned out his room. She tried to remain positive and upbeat for his sake, but his pain was her pain, and it was difficult to see him without a smile on his face.

Nicolette was only able to get a word here and there from Pastor Wright's sermon, which was on The Blessings of Abraham. Friday night she'd wowed both herself and Darian by praying with so much power, that the presence of God could be felt among them, as her grandmother had done with her and her sister so many times before.

The only thing missing in the church that was familiar to her was Darian. She'd called him that morning with no answer, and assumed he'd gone to church early, but once service began she realized he was not there. It took all of her strength to remain seated and not leave the church in search of him, still she counted the minutes until worship service would be over.

She closed her eyes, and as Pastor Wright prayed she prayed that Darian was alright, and before he could say Amen good she was out of her seat rushing for the exit, as were other churchgoers eager to get out and back into the world.

"Nikki," Adrian snatched her arm before she could exit the sanctuary. "Have you seen my brother?"

"No," she pulled away and walked out into the church foyer.

"Come down the hall with me, my father wanted me to grab you before you left," he pulled her towards the hallway and she reluctantly followed.

"Nikki where's Darian?" Pastor Wright came at her with an accusatory tone as though she were the reason he was not present.

"I don't know," Nicolette shrugged. "I was going to look for him when I left here."

"Where's my baby?" Evelyn barged into the office slamming the door behind her.

"I haven't seen him today," Nicolette responded.

"What do you mean you haven't seen him?" Evelyn demanded.

"I left him at his apartment last night, and when I called him this morning his phone was off, so I assumed he'd left for church early."

"Well he hasn't been here," Evelyn and Pastor Wright exchanged confused looks.

"I see," Nicolette didn't like the way the Wrights were looking at her.

"Did the two of you have a fight last night?" Evelyn wanted to know.

"No," Nicolette wondered what that had to do with anything.

"Then why did you go home?" Evelyn gave her a doubtful stare.

"That's where all my stuff is," she spat.

"So you don't live with Darian?"

The suggestion made Nicolette want to slap Evelyn. She'd had about enough of this uppity, adulterous, hussy, "of course not! Darian is a faithful servant of the Lord, there's no way I'd allow him to do anything to negate that."

"Oh," Evelyn looked surprised. "I just assumed that since the two of you are always together you…"

"I get it," Nicolette scowled. "The pregnant whore who's stealing your son got him to propose by sleeping with him. I mean we are all adults here, and surely I've been in his bed, why else would he want to marry me right?"

"Nikki I-I didn't say that," Evelyn's face turned red.

"You didn't have to," Nicolette shook her head. "You already told me the only reason you hired me was to keep an eye on me. My relationship with your son is a spiritual journey, something you church folks may never understand."

"Forget all this, it's not the time!" Adrian fussed. "Even if you're not living with my brother you're his fiancé, the least you could have done was go by and check on him this morning after what he went through."

"The least I could do?" Nicolette got in Adrian's face. "The least I could do was sit with Darian for hours when he was at the

Emergency Vet with Midnight, and I did. The least I could do was be a shoulder for Darian to cry on when he faced the reality that Midnight was gone, and I was. The least I could do was hold his hand as he watched something he loved be committed to the ground forever, and I was right there holding his hand! Where were you? You didn't even know Midnight was buried yesterday because you were not there! No visits, no phone calls, nothing!"

"Nikki calm down," Pastor Wright caressed her shoulder but her temper was hotter than jalapeno peppers dipped in habanera sauce.

"Now I understand why Darian says some of the things he says about his family. Church folks spend so much time trying to look good, that they don't know what it is to really do good. To be by someone's side when they are hurt like a true Christian, to comfort, and pray for them."

"I do pray for my son," Pastor Wright objected.

"Still Darian thinks you all don't care about him, he said it out of his own mouth. The reason he feels that way is because instead of giving him the love and support he needs you expect him to be alright. He may not feel good at times, but he always looks good, and that's all you seem to care about." She gestured towards Adrian, "so you focus all of your energy on making that heathen over there look good instead of giving your efforts to the one who may need it the most."

"Let me tell you something!" Evelyn hollered.

"No," Nicolette shook her head. "Put whatever feeling you may or may not have towards me aside and go comfort your son," she turned and let herself out of the office.

"Nikki wait!" Adrian caught up with her as she reached the front of the church and quickly gained the attention of the stragglers and gossipers still at the church.

"What do you want?" Nicolette asked.

"I want to go with you, I wanted to call him, you have to believe I did. I wanted to go by and see him, but I couldn't. I just didn't know what to say to him," Adrian looked as though he wanted to cry.

"Do you think I knew what to say? All I knew was he needed someone and I was going to be there."

"I'm sorry," he hugged Nicolette. "I'm sorry I wasn't there, I was afraid alright."

"You don't owe me anything, but your brother needs you. Sometimes when no words seem appropriate your presence is enough."

"Can I go with you to his apartment?" Adrian looked hopeful.

"Yeah," Nicolette smiled. "That would be nice."

"Let's go," Adrian took Nicolette's hand and led her to his truck leaving the remaining congregation with something to talk about.

"Are you serious?" Adrian laughed as he pulled in front of Darian's apartment. "Well we're here I'll call you in a few," he hung up the phone. "You won't believe what someone just called my mom and told her," he said as they got out of the truck.

"Do I even want to know?" At this point Nicolette had already come to the conclusion that there were plenty of liars in the church and not much surprised her anymore.

"They said that we were hugging and kissing in front of the church, then we got into my truck and left," he shook his head as they approached the door.

"People have nothing better to do," Nicolette rang Darian's doorbell.

"Tell me about it," he huffed.

Darian opened the door and immediately embraced Nicolette, "hey, I'm glad you came by."

"What's up man?" Adrian asked.

"You could have left him where he was," Darian glared at his brother as he released Nicolette and they entered the apartment.

"Don't be like that," Adrian shook his head.

"I have nothing to say to you," Darian took Nicolette's hand and led her to the living room. "I got something for the baby."

"Where were you this morning?" Nicolette demanded to know.

"I overslept," he gave a nonchalant shrug. "But I got a lot of stuff for the baby."

"Darian I get it man. I wasn't there for you and I'm sorry," Adrian apologized.

"Did you figure that one out all by yourself or did Nikki lay a good guilt trip on you?"

Adrian didn't respond.

"Just like I thought," he shook his head. "You are selfish, never there at the church when you're supposed to be. Never there for anyone but yourself."

"Don't try to play that high and mighty crap with me Darian. You might have saved the day in mom and dad's eyes by getting engaged to a pregnant woman who had no man to care for her and her unborn child, but newsflash, Nikki would have been just fine without you."

"You don't know anything about her, you've never tried."

"Nikki he's done his share of dirt," Adrian gave him a malicious grin. "Just because he hasn't been in your bed don't make him a virgin Nikki. As a matter of fact it sounds like there must be a leak in here."

"She already knows," Darian shook his head.

"Drip, drip, drip."

"Get out!" Darian hollered.

"Why don't you tell your future wife about the gift you got from your friend Crystal for your eighteenth birthday?"

"I already did," Darian nodded. "*No weapons formed against me shall prosper.*"

"Preach on preacher!" Adrian hooted. "You're nothing but a scripture quoting hypocrite!"

"*Every tongue that accuses me in judgment He will condemn,*" Darian put his finger in Adrian's face.

"*Let he who is without sin cast the first stone!*" Adrian pushed his brother's hand away.

"*Judge not lest ye be judged!*"

"*He who covers and forgives an offense seeks love, but he who repeats or harps on a matter separates even close friends,*" Adrian shook his head. "How about that one oh mighty righteous brother who can't forgive his brother for making a mistake!"

"A brother looks out for you, your struggle is his struggle, your grief is his grief," Darian sighed.

"Is that really in the Bible?" Adrian asked.

"Nah, that's in my heart."

"I'm sorry," Adrian opened his arms and his brother embraced him.

"So are you coming to my wedding?" Darian pulled away.

"Of course, when is it?"

"Sometime in the next two weeks," Darian avoided making eye contact with Nicolette who was standing with her mouth wide open.

"I wouldn't miss it man," he smiled with pride. "Congratulations!"

"Thank you," Darian beamed as if nothing had ever gone wrong between the two of them.

"Do you need anything, is there anything I can do?"

"No, but thanks for dropping her off, I'll take her to get her car later," Darian opened his front door and all but pushed his brother outside.

"I'll call you tonight bro, bye Nikki," he said before Darian shut the door in his face.

"Nothing like spiritual warfare huh?" Nicolette shook her head.

"Do you want to get married tomorrow?" He took her hand and caressed it gently.

"You're not going to get off the hook that easily," Nicolette huffed. "Why weren't you at church this morning?"

"Because I had it out with God this morning, I lost of course. Now I understand why things had to turn out the way they did, and I'm ready to move on."

"Wait a minute. What do you mean had it out with God? You make it sound like you had a boxing match."

"Actually I kind of did, and He knocked me out with one blow. I grabbed a Bible, which subsequently was yours. I looked up and demanded that God make me understand. When I opened the Bible I opened it to the page you marked as your favorite scripture."

"Ecclesiastes 3?"

"Yep, I've read it before, but knowing that it touched your heart made me look at it in a new light. There was one part in particular that really got to me," he sighed.

"A *time to be born and a time to die*?"

"No, verse three, *A time to break down, and a time to build up*. I broke down, but I can't stay there," he shook his head with confidence. "I have to pick up the pieces of my life and build it up. I want to build my life with you and this baby, no more waiting, no more doubts. Friday night I was angry with God, I didn't care that I knew right from wrong, I wanted to do my own will. I really need to pick up your Bible more often, I flipped to the new testament and ended up back in Ephesians where I read the fifth chapter and when I started to read I felt guilty for what I tried to do not just to myself, but to you. If I'm going to lead this marriage then I can't lead us both into hell because I'm upset."

"I can make my own decisions."

"But God wants me to lead you, and I'm sorry I lost my head and tried to pull you in the wrong direction," he embraced her. "I'm ready to start my life with you. To build up a marriage, a family, a home," he hugged her again.

"And you got all this from opening the Bible to two random pages?"

"Yes," he released her and held her hands.

"Are you sure you were not called to be a preacher?"

"I don't know," he shrugged.

"So what about your parents, are you upset with them?"

"No," he placed his hand on Nicolette's shoulder. "I called them right after you left the church. My mom told me about how you called all of them out for not being there for me. They both apologized and I can't stay mad at them, I love them too much, and life is too short."

"So why were you so hot with Adrian?"

"I wasn't," he shrugged. "I just like picking fights with him. That's what we do."

"So what now?"

"We plan a wedding," he kissed her hand.

Chapter Twelve

"It's official," Darian smiled at his father as he watched Nicolette and Evelyn hug.

"Son I'm proud of you," Pastor Wright beamed. "Now if only we could get this one under control," he shifted his eyes towards Adrian.

"Hey wifey material ain't easy to find," Adrian argued.

"To find something first you have to start looking for it," Evelyn told him.

"I am looking," his comment caught the entire family off guard. "Who knew this clown would get married before me?"

"Don't worry you'll find someone," Darian embraced Nicolette. "My wife and I will pray about it."

"I love you," Nicolette whispered in his ear before pulling away.

"I love you more," Darian kissed her and they felt as if no one else in the world existed.

"Excuse me," Adrian tapped his brother on the shoulder. "Nobody wants to see all that."

"You don't understand," Darian released Nicolette and turned to his brother. "The feeling of holding a woman and knowing that she's your wife is just something I can't describe."

"Oh I can think of quite a few words that can describe what you're feeling, I just can't say them in front of mom and dad," he chuckled. "And you don't have to worry about birth control for the first few months."

"Adrian it's not physical. So many men try to make love a physical thing and miss out on the real feeling."

"Whipped!" Adrian shook his head. "Are you sure you two haven't—"

"Shut up Adrian!" Evelyn and Darian shouted.

"Boy what is wrong with you?" Pastor Wright asked.

"I'm honest, I can't help it. It's a benefit to being a preacher's kid," Adrian grinned.

"Something must have gone horribly wrong in the womb with this one," Darian nodded in his brother's direction.

"I hate to just skip out on you," Pastor Wright glanced at his watch. "Evelyn and I have another engagement to be to so we need to get going. Make sure Adrian leaves before the two of you do and lock up for me."

"Yes sir," Darian responded as he put his arm around Nicolette.

"Congratulations young lady," Pastor Wright hugged Nicolette and it was the first time she'd recalled being embraced by him. "Welcome to the family."

Evelyn kissed her son, "I'm proud of you."

"Thanks," he beamed as his parents exited.

"There are going to be a lot of angry women in church tomorrow morning when you show up with a wedding band on Darian," Adrian huffed.

"After the rumor that got started about me and Adrian kissing in front of the church last Sunday this should really give them something to talk about," Nicolette giggled. As far as the gossiping members of the church knew Nicolette was carrying Darian's child, and as far as they were concerned that was all they needed to know.

"I guess I'll be getting out of here too," Adrian exhaled.

"We're right behind you," Darian cheesed.

"I'm happy for you," Adrian extended his hand towards his little brother.

"Thanks, that means a lot," Darian shook his brother's hand.

"Can a brother have ten dollars gas money?" Adrian asked innocently.

Darian and Nicolette exchanged glances, "Nikki I'll be back let me walk him to his truck."

"Okay, I'm going to the guest room to change out of this dress. I'm freezing," she shivered.

"I love you," Darian put his arms around Nicolette.

"I love you too," she kissed him on the cheek.

"Come on girl we just got married, you have to do better than that," he tilted her head and kissed her on the lips. "You know this will be the first time since we've been married that we won't be in the same room together."

"Boy you better come on here and stop with all that!" Adrian pulled his brother from Nicolette's embrace. "I'll holla Nikki."

"Bye Adrian," Nicolette turned and headed to the guest room. She stood in front of the full length mirror on the door and looked at herself in the white dress Evelyn had insisted on buying for her. It wasn't quite her taste, but it made Evelyn happy. Nicolette was so in love with Darian it wouldn't have mattered if she'd married him naked.

She began to rub her round six month pregnant belly. She had been jittery and nervous all day, but the baby was as calm as a river throughout the entire exchange of vows. Now that it was over she felt like the baby was trying to knock a hole in her stomach.

"Knock, knock," Darian opened the door and she took a step back.

"That was quick," she smiled up at him.

"What did you expect? You just told me you were about to come in here and get naked," he pulled her in to him and kissed her brow.

"You know your mother is a super sleuth so you better get whatever thought is going through your mind out with the quickness," she tried to pull away and he held her tighter.

"On a serious note though, I know we never discussed it, but if you don't feel comfortable we don't have to do anything before the baby is born. I'm a patient man, I can wait a few months. We have a long life ahead of us," he kissed her brow again. "Unless of course the good Lord decides to try to be funny and take me out of this world within the next few months."

"Nicolette Lillian Wright," she said her new name with a smile.

"Baby?"

"Huh?" Nicolette asked holding back on her urge to laugh at him.

"You didn't answer me," he exhaled.

"Answer you? What do you mean?"

He cleared his throat, "I said we don't have to do anything if you don't want to, but you never said whether you want to or not."

"You said you are a patient man," she stated with a straight face.

"I am," he said with waning confidence.

"So you'll have to be patient, and wait until later to find out," she kissed him.

"Aw come on Nikki," he whined. "Tell me something."

"I will," she removed his hand from behind her back and placed it on her belly just in time for him to feel the baby kick. "In due season."

"Now that we're married and your issues are my issues I have a little issue I need you to help me with," his seriousness made her nervous.

"What?"

"I need you to help me tell my dad I'm taking a semester off."

"No you're not," Nicolette stated authoritatively.

"I can work with this guy from the choir to save up extra money, and I'll be able to spend time at home after the baby is born."

"There's no way your parents will go for that anyway," she shook her head.

"They don't have a choice, it's kind of a done deal," he sighed. "I kind of spent the tuition money I had saved up for next semester on your engagement ring."

"You shouldn't have gotten me a ring, you should have just asked me to marry you."

"Girl," he looked at her like she was stupid. "My mother is Evelyn Wright, she don't play that."

"Unzip me," she turned her back to him and allowed him to unzip her dress. "Now look away."

"We are married now," he informed her with a grin.

"And we are in your momma's house, she is a super sleuth. Ain't nothing going on in this house," Nikki began to change her clothes.

"I am so blessed," he sighed as he stared at his wife. "I've prayed for this day and I can't believe it's finally here."

"What God has for you is for you that's for sure, I never thought I'd be in a place like this. And the best part about it is that there is no place where I'd rather be."

Chapter Thirteen

"He is so adorable," Evelyn cooed over the newborn as he rested in Nicolette's arms.

"Son he looks just like you," Pastor Wright looked back and forth between the baby and Darian.

"He's a newborn, everyone knows newborn babies don't look like anyone at first," Adrian provided his uninvited words of wisdom.

"Let me hold him," it was a command not a question, but everyone knew to expect nothing less from Evelyn Wright as she took baby Darnel from his mother's arms.

"Grandma Evelyn," Adrian chuckled.

"Oh no sir! I am not grandma. I don't know what I am yet, but I can't be nobody's grandma. I'm much too sophisticated for such a title."

"I could have told you she wasn't going to go for that one," Darian grinned.

"Darius look at this," Evelyn nudged her husband.

"Mom why are you undressing him, it's cold in here," Darian protested.

"Son is there something you want to tell us?" The accusatory look Pastor Wright gave him made Nicolette's heart skip a beat.

"No why?"

"Nikki did you see this?" Evelyn pointed to the birthmark on the baby's shoulder.

"Yeah it's a birthmark," Nicolette informed them.

"You've been married to my son for three months, I know you've seen his naked behind by now."

"Mom!" Darian shouted.

"What?" She asked innocently. "Don't tell me you didn't notice this baby has the exact same birth mark you have on your butt."

"Actually I didn't," Darian stood over his mother and looked down at the baby. "I didn't even know her when…"

"Busted!" Adrian sang the word.

"I swear," Darian placed his hand over his mouth in awe.

"This is not possible," Nicolette reasoned.

"All of you are putting way too much thought into this," Pastor Wright chuckled. "If Darian and Nicolette never met before this child was conceived then God must have a pretty awesome plan."

"Don't let him off that easy," Adrian sucked his teeth. "At least make him take a paternity test."

"It doesn't matter if I take ten, this baby is mine!" Darian roared.

"Calm down son," Pastor Wright warned. "You don't want to scare the baby. Besides we all know how much your family means to you."

"Oh Nikki," Darian sighed. "I'm so sorry, I didn't mean—"

"Darian it's okay really, I know you love him," Nicolette shook her head with confidence as Evelyn gently caressed the baby's cheek.

"I hate to be the one to break up this joyous occasion, but I have to go," Adrian interrupted.

"Where are you headed?" Evelyn asked.

"I have a doctor's appointment," he sighed.

"Adrian?" Darian gave him a disappointed look.

"No bro, I think the nurse there likes me though. She's well worth the fifteen dollar co-pay."

"So you're going to the doctor for no reason?"

"Hey a brother needs a checkup every now and then. If I'm dying I want to be the first to know."

"Do you need gas money?" Pastor Wright reached for his wallet.

"Nah, I got it taken care of," he waved before backing out of the room.

"Well that's a first," Pastor Wright returned his wallet to his back pocket.

"Here go to your mom," Evelyn placed the baby back in his mother's arms.

"Man labor is rough," Darian huffed. "I thought I was going to die after all that pushing."

"What are you complaining about Nikki was the one pushing."

"Man I pushed too, I couldn't help it. This little boy is as stubborn as his mother because he didn't want to come out."

"It was horrible, I can't believe you went through that twice," Nikki told Evelyn.

"By the time we're done you're going to go through it at least three of four more times," Darian said with a straight face.

"Is that your way of volunteering to give birth next time?"

"Look at him baby, it was worth it," Darian smiled with pride.

"Not when I thought I was going to be getting an epidural."

"Why didn't you get it?" Evelyn asked.

"The doctor wouldn't give it to her because she has a tattoo on her back. He didn't want the ink to get into her bloodstream," Darian explained.

"The things you kids do to your bodies," Pastor Wright chuckled.

"I didn't know you had tattoos," Evelyn looked horrified.

"Neither did I," Darian raised his hand.

Evelyn and Pastor Wright looked at their son.

"What I didn't, she's shy," he explained.

"Shy?" Evelyn laughed.

"Yes, when she came to work in mismatched shoes it wasn't because she couldn't see her feet, it was because she gets dressed in the dark."

"I don't like people to stare at me," Nicolette stated.

"I need to talk to you when you get a minute son," Darian's father gave him a once over and everyone knew he wanted to ask if they'd consummated their marriage.

"As my father or as my pastor?"

"Well…both," he shrugged.

"She married me for love," he assured his father kissing his wife on the forehead.

"We need to be heading back to the church, but call us if you need us," Pastor Wright glanced at his watch.

"I love you dad," Darian embraced his father. "I hope I can be as great a father to Darnel as you are to me."

"I have no doubt you will be," he hugged his son.

"Thank you both for everything," Darian released his father and took a step back.

"I thank God for you everyday son," Pastor Wright opened the door and allowed Evelyn to exit and he followed.

"I guess at times like this you learn to count your blessings," Darian smiled at Nicolette.

"I guess so," Nicolette agreed with a smile.

"Come here little man," Darian cradled baby Darnel in his arms. "I can't promise you to be perfect, but I can promise to always be there for you. I love you and your mom with all my heart. I'll do whatever it takes to make sure you know that."

"I don't know how I would have made it through all this without you."

"And you'll never have to wonder Miss I Don't Need Anyone," Darian chuckled.

"I love you," Nicolette smiled at her other half.

"I love you too," he beamed back. "You are everything I ever wanted in a woman."

"I guess it's true, what is meant to be will be."

"To everything there is a season," Darian kissed Nicolette and held his son close. She knew in her heart that she was truly blessed, and there was no better feeling.

Made in the USA
Lexington, KY
15 February 2014